THE HIGH SEA CONSPIRACY

Manveen S Anand

OM
Om Books International

First published in 2015 by

OM

Om Books International

Corporate & Editorial Office
A-12, Sector 64, Noida 201 301
Uttar Pradesh, India
Phone: +91 120 477 4100
Email: editorial@ombooks.com
Website: www.ombooksinternational.com

Sales Office
107, Ansari Road, Darya Ganj,
New Delhi 110 002, India
Phone: +91 11 2326 3363, 2326 5303, 4000 9000
Fax: +91 11 2327 8091
Email: sales@ombooks.com
Website: www.ombooks.com

ISBN: 978-93-83202-21-8

Printed in India

10 9 8 7 6 5 4 3 2 1

Contents

To my parents
for all their support and guidance

1

Escape From Recife

Twenty-six-year-old Ricardo lived alone in the small town of Recife in North Brazil. Abandoned by his mother when he was a child, Ricardo was taken in by his cousin, Marco, who he believed, was from his father's side. But there's no knowing that for sure. Then one fine morning, Marco was gone. Just vanished without a trace, leaving little Ricardo on the streets.

Mercifully, he was taken in by English missionaries who ran an orphanage, and would spend many years of his life there with other destitute for company and learning.

A grown-up Ricardo set many hearts aflutter. Strong, large-framed, the young man with thick black hair and blue eyes, for the locals, was a clean-hearted person, never broke any law, never wronged anyone. He didn't have many friends, rarely spoke and kept largely to himself. He spoke good English though—probably picked it up at the orphanage. He may even have gotten it from his mother, but was she English? No one ever spoke to him about his parents.

And soon it was payback time. The orphanage fixed up Ricardo with a merchant navy company called International Marine, to work as a navigator. Delighted at first when he was informed about his training, Ricardo thought he would finally get away from the burdensome memories of Recife. But the orphanage made him sign a contract—he would have to train in Recife and pay all the money he earned to the orphanage. In return, he would get a monthly stipend of 10 per cent of his earnings. Fair deal.

Bondage was acceptable if it could take him away from his prison for a few months every now and then. But that could not be a permanent arrangement.

~

It was a quiet dawn in Recife. The air was still and the sun crept out reluctantly. Ricardo's room was like a cabin in a cheap highway motel. Standing rain water had seeped through the ceiling, now full of damp patches. Uneven walls matched the peeling paint. The only furniture in the room was a rickety folding bed and a small wooden computer table with a stool.

Ricardo usually slept here with his head buried under a pillow, insulating himself from the noise of the world preparing itself for each new day. But this morning was different; the noise was in his room. The vibrations of his cell phone, lost between the sheets, woke him up with a start. He grabbed the set and peering at it through half-opened eyes, and pressed a button he thought was the right one.

'Hello…,' he said lazily. Suddenly he was wide awake, like a prey making a final dash for life. He was being deputed on an important mission and would have to be off in 24 hours. That was a tall order but he was in no position to disobey. In fact, he didn't want to. Rubbing his sleep-starved eyes, he immediately called International Marine.

A voice answered, 'This is Steven. How may I help you?'

'Steven, it's Ricardo.'

'Oh, good morning. How's it going? Ready to join?'

'Yes,' he replied and added, 'I'll join the *Castle.*'

After a minute's banter, he hung up with little or no idea of what was in store for him.

~

Ricardo sauntered along the busy suburban sidewalk swinging a small backpack bloated with his gym accessories. His mind was trying to find a way back home. He was perplexed by the call that had woken him up that morning. '*Castle*,' the man on the other side had repeatedly said in a hushed tone. The word kept running in his head like a breaking news ticker on a prime-time television programme. It was too big a decision to take by himself. He needed advice, a green signal, but from whom?

Lost in thought, he walked past a strange sight on the sidewalk. Turning back, Ricardo saw an old man, probably in his eighties, sitting cross-legged on a small brick structure, his long unkempt hair flying about his face. A torn white shirt exposed his bony shoulders, and an off-white sheet was wrapped around his waist—the shrivelled man looked like a character from a Gothic tale. Three tarot cards lay neatly spread on a sheet in front of him.

'Your mind seems to be playing tricks with your soul today,' said the old man in a sing-song accent as he smiled.

Ricardo bent down to meet the mystic's gaze. The old man said, 'Pick a card, son.'

Without saying a word, Ricardo picked the card in the centre of the row.

Even before he could look at it, the old man snatched it from his hand. The expression on his face hardened into a mix of anger and fear. He looked deep into Ricardo's eyes and said softly, 'What you set forth on is against your will. No wonder your mind encounters opposition. But the cards have turned.'

And then he added in a barely audible whisper, 'But the fog shall lift soon.'

As Ricardo resumed sauntering along the sidewalk, with the backpack slung on his shoulder, the words of the old man echoed in his head.

~

By late evening, Ricardo was at the beach, lazing on a mattress. Torso exposed, he was in quarter-length cargoes. Everything around him seemed still. There was no wind unsettling the grains of sand. A little boy wondered how to preserve a sand castle, while a young couple sat near the edge, with their arms around each other. The water was crystal clear. The beauty of the sun melting into the sea banished all morbid thoughts. Ricardo stared at the skies and the sea.

And then the thoughts returned to assail him again. He was perplexed. He was struggling, trying to convince himself of his decision. As the last bit of light was swallowed up by darkness, Ricardo got up and started walking towards the small open air bar at the end of the beach.

A huge poster hung outside with 'Brahma' scrawled on it. Make no mistake, this Brahma was a beer major in South America.

Ricardo knew Venus, the bartender. What an odd name for a bartender, he thought. A tall dark-skinned man with short brown hair and deep black eyes, Venus looked more like a bouncer than a bartender. Though he never mentioned anything to Ricardo, he had heard about Ricardo—Chinese whispers at the bar, and such whispers are seldom ballads.

Ricardo entered the bar and made himself comfortable. A regular wooden structure with no frills, the bar had a huge refrigerator stacked with beer, and a few bottles of untouched local liquor on a wooden shelf behind the refrigerator.

Usually Venus greeted Ricardo with, 'Hey there, sad to see you alone again. Staying in that cubby hole, you can't get a girl man, face it!'

And Ricardo would retort, 'I'll have a beer and nice to see you with all those girls in the bar.'

Today Ricardo was too caught up in his thoughts and didn't even hear what Venus said.

Venus greeted him loudly this time, 'Hey there! You look worked up man, what's up?'

'Nothing much. Long day, I guess,' Ricardo replied.

'Yeah right, as if you had something to do.'

Ricardo was taken in by surprise. 'Do you even know what I do?'

'Do I look like I care?' Venus spat back. 'Anyway you look like you need a new life.'

Ricardo didn't reply. He let Venus's last line sink in slowly. Then a faint smile appeared on his lips. He looked at Venus with a twinkle in his eyes. 'You're right, buddy,' he said softly, 'I do need a new life!'

This was not what Venus had expected to hear. But before he could think of a fresh offensive, Ricardo chucked two Brazilian reals on the table, hopped off the bar stool, and left without looking back.

2

A Bid Unchallenged

In the southern city of Kingston, Jamaica, it was a quiet day with a cool sea breeze blowing.

The young lad drove down an empty two-lane road on a single-seat scooter with 'Pizza Boy' written in bold letters on the back. His orange top and white baggy cargoes complimented his mood as he sang native songs loudly. He slowed down as he approached a massive iron gate at the end of the lane. Multi-coloured vine had claimed most of the ferrous curlicues, lending the imposing frame a sinister heaviness. A hidden camera monitored the world outside the gate while a small speaker was neatly fixed into an adjacent wall.

Parking his scooter at a distance, the delivery boy coolly walked up to the gate and peered at the huge mansion on the other side. Suddenly, two Rottweilers came charging out of nowhere, barking loudly as they flew at the gate. Biting and scratching the clanging structure mercilessly, they pressed forward towards their hunt.

The delivery boy was caught off-guard. Startled, he fell back on the road, dropping the boxes. Before he could gather his wits, the speaker on the wall came alive.

'Who is it?' a harsh voice demanded.

The terrified boy looked again at the wild dogs still trying to make it past the iron barrier, and leapt to his feet. Gone was his joyous mood as he approached the device and positioned himself in front of it.

'You order a pizza, man,' he said in a typical Jamaican accent.

Before he could say anything more, a small entrance in the huge gate swung open with a creaking noise. He jumped back anticipating a canine attack but nothing happened. The dogs had disappeared. Cautiously he moved towards the small entrance, measuring his steps for any sign of danger. An armed guard was sitting a few metres away holding the two attackers. To the boy's surprise, the animals were totally docile.

'Them creatures almost gave me a heart attack!'

The guard smiled, patting the dogs. 'That way,' he said, pointing towards the mansion.

The boy started walking hastily towards it and shouted back, 'You sure you ain't got more of those inside?'

At the main entrance, another armed guard came out, handed over the bill money, and almost snatched the box from his hand.

'Keep the change.'

And just when he was about to go inside, he turned and said with a smirk, 'We let the dogs free in one minute.'

Alarmed at his words, the boy managed a faint smile before making a dash for the exit.

The guard chuckled to himself perversely as he closed the main entrance door behind him. Pizza boxes in hand, he walked into a huge hall. The floor was laid with expensive Italian marble; the walls had huge teak windows covered with off-white sheers swaying to the breeze. The ceiling was evenly painted in Baroque style. Ming vases adorned the corners. From the centre of the hall, a wooden staircase led to the next level.

The guard went up the staircase into an open lobby decorated like the hall. In the centre lay a huge sofa on which a middle-aged man sat comfortably. Tro—that was the name he went by. He had earned it during his days in the Philippines. With his tanned skin and fine built, he looked unmistakably South American. Dressed in a white linen shirt and trousers, his closely cropped hair, graying at the sides, matched his clothes.

Two beautiful ladies sat on either side, each holding a glass of champagne. Armed guards lined the lobby, ready for an encounter. One of them walked up to him holding out a cell phone. 'Tro, call from the party,' he whispered.

Tro took the phone from the guard casually and without moving from the sofa, pressed it to his ear. 'Hello General Lee, good you wish to bid for the data. This deal is worth it,' he said in a typical Latin accent. He listened for a few seconds before saying coldly, 'That is not possible. I have given my word. There will be a bid. The time and location will be communicated to you soon.' He got up and added in a serious tone, 'The data belongs to the highest bidder. It's as simple as that. And fair game too.'

Then hanging up, he looked at the clear skies above, and smiled softly as he inhaled the cool breeze.

~

In the Chinese town of Rizhao, no one stayed up late. Everyone turned in early. No late walkers whatsoever, probably because of the local mafia. They kept everyone indoors. The streets were completely deserted. Even the light from the austere street lamps was barely enough to see anyone standing beneath.

Two guards dressed in neat black suits stood at the entrance to a club. Dimly lit by an overhead lamp was a board that said 'Shong Si'. The same words were inscribed below in Mandarin. Suddenly tearing through the darkness, two bright lights raced towards the club. The deep jagged scar across the face of one of the guards shone brightly.

A black Mercedes slowly rolled up the street. Before the car could come to a halt, two men dressed in dull green uniforms wearing peak caps of the same colour, jumped out of it and positioned themselves in front of a rear door of the car, now in front of the entrance. Unmistakably, the Chinese police.

The two guards standing outside the club moved closer to each other, blocking the entrance.

The rear door of the car opened noiselessly and a middle-aged Chinese in a spotless black suit with a purple shirt stepped out. He was a little shorter than his bodyguards but from his carriage and gait, he was a clear superior. General Kin Lee was General of the regional police. The moment he stepped out, his sentinels closed rank around him, blocking him off from view. As they neared the entrance, the club guards stood firmly in the way. Their message was clear, 'All other cops stay out.'

The General signalled his men who immediately backed off. The two club guards opened up just enough space between them for the General to pass.

As he entered the club, he was greeted by another group of guards. From a dark corner, a young Chinese girl walked up to him, majestically holding a silver tray covered with a bright red cloth. Stopping in front of the

General, she lowered her head to avoid eye contact—a traditional way of showing respect to the powerful. The General looked at the young girl and without a change of expression, pulled out his pistol and placed it on the tray.

As the girl stepped back to leave, one of the guards stepped forward and pointing to a small passage, said in Mandarin, 'This way, General.'

They entered a plush room decorated with traditional Chinese art. By the dim light, it was difficult to take in too many details. In the middle lay a table with seats occupied on all sides. The General walked up to the last vacant seat and sat down quietly. None of the faces in the room were visible, just an array of shadowy heads.

Without warning, someone pressed a button. A small overhead light came on. Tro was sitting erect in an off-white suit with his shirt unbuttoned at the chest. He looked around—some of the most influential mafias, cartels and Yakuzas in the world were in the room ready to participate in a secret covenant, as it were.

'Good evening gentlemen.' Tro greeted the guests with a faint smile. 'As we all know, we have gathered here for the bidding of the data. You have already indicated your intentions and amounts. After I reveal the highest bid, you will be given a last chance to outbid that amount, if you so desire.'

He waited for a while, scrutinising the shadows and added, 'I should also tell you that the market value of the data is estimated to be much higher than what we estimate.'

There was a deathly silence in the room. No one seemed to breathe. Tro pulled out a small paper from his pocket. 'The final bid stands at USD 2 billion.'

He paused before speaking again, 'Anybody wants to reconsider his bid? We have 10 minutes for that.'

No one moved or said a word. Finally Tro got up from his seat and said, 'Very well then, this meeting is over.'

As people slowly trickled out of the room, Tro and the General stayed back. From the way things had turned out, it seemed the General would take home the prized data.

3

On Board MV *Castle*

Ricardo had packed and was ready to leave Recife again. He was ready to walk into an uncertain future which could not have been any worse than his past.

Motor Vessel *Castle* was a 199-metres bulk carrier registered in Panama, but had nothing to do with that nation. That's how it is in the merchant navy world. Every ship complies with regulations set internationally by the United Nations offshoot, 'International Maritime Organisation', commonly known as the IMO.

That's not all. Every country whips up additional regulations for vessels registered on their land to catch them out for non-compliance, and makes a killing in the process. But some countries don't really bother to make any more regulations. In fact, they don't bother about the existing ones either. These countries, marked as ports of convenience to degrade their reputation, are a hit with ship owners. Understandably.

Ricardo was to join from Paraguay. He was given a train ticket by the company to make it on time before the ship set sail. No one came to see him off. He arrived alone at the station in a taxi. In his well-fitting T-shirt and a pair of cargoes, he looked every bit a true rugged traveller. Families gathered on the platform to say goodbye to their loved ones. Mothers kissed and hugged their children before seeing them off. And the elderly, as usual, dispensed vital advice nobody was interested in.

Ricardo paid the cabbie a few extra Brazilian reals for the ride. Why not? After all he was the only one there to bid him goodbye. Ricardo boarded the train and found his seat in a corner. Dumping his worn-out travel bag on the overhead rack, he slumped into his seat and took a deep breath as he tried to distance himself from that black hole called Recife.

As he tried to purge himself of his past, the man on the adjacent seat butted in with a heavy voice, 'Good day friend, going to Paraguay?'

The man, probably in his late thirties, with the odd gray hair in an otherwise black crop, was neatly dressed in formals. His face seemed finely hewn out of a rock. With a crew cut and clean-shaven face, he looked like a sophisticated businessman.

'Yes,' replied Ricardo, trying to keep his answer short to avoid sustained interrogation.

'Business or holiday?' the man persisted.

With a forced smile, Ricardo inquired politely, 'Sorry to ask, but you are…?'

'Carlos… Inspector José Carlos.'

The biggest fear in Brazil, after thanatophobia, is the phobia of cops.

Ricardo was slightly taken aback. 'Oh, sorry… I'm Ricardo, Ricardo Pablo… Inspector.'

'It's ok, you can call me Carlos. I'm not that formal,' he said with a smile. Ricardo could tell that was a lie as his clothes gave him away.

During the three-hour journey to Paraguay, Ricardo found a new friend and learnt much about the police. Carlos was the chief of special operations in North Brazil and wielded the kind of power most youth in the country just dreamt of. In short, he was a powerful man and now he was a friend.

Ricardo told him about his upcoming voyage onboard the *Castle* and life in Recife. Odd as it may seem, he opened up his life to a stranger. He had never done that before. Perhaps he needed the comforting presence of a perfect stranger to do so. But he didn't speak about Marco. He didn't feel the need to.

Before they knew, the train was pulling into the station at Paraguay. As they got off, Carlos gave him his business card. 'Well then, Ricardo, it was nice meeting you,' he said.

'I'll definitely keep in touch. And show me that gun some day,' Ricardo said as they both laughed.

Ricardo held the card in his hand. He had found a friend. Glancing across the platform, he spotted Carlos with a tall beautiful girl dressed in a black formal outfit and pencil heels. They seemed to be exchanging some information which did not seem to please the inspector too much.

Suddenly, Ricardo saw a man holding up a placard with his name. The aged man with the welcoming smile was the company's driver.

Ricardo walked up to him and greeted him warmly. 'That's me you're looking for,' he confirmed as he handed over his sack. Then he turned to look across the platform for Carlos and the lady, but they had disappeared.

Ricardo got into an old Mercedes Wagon. A Spanish song played on the radio. The port was about an hour's drive from the station. Through the ride, Ricardo's mind wavered between Recife and the landscape outside framed by the car window. The chauffeur slowed down as he entered the port limits. The port was a huge expanse with a large belt rolling out of a refinery at one corner, heading steadily towards the wharf.

They drove across the refinery, passing under the belt, when suddenly without warning, the driver hit the brakes. Ricardo was jolted out of his reverie.

'That's her,' said the driver pointing towards a huge black-hulled cargo ship. From the end of the quay, Ricardo could see 'MV *Castle*' written in life- sized letters at the stern. Indeed, she looked like a huge floating castle. Held to the wharf with four ropes on the front and four at the stern, she was longer than what Ricardo had expected. The hull was a majestic and stately black. The four-storeyed structure at the stern was the living quarters. A number of antennas stretched skyward from atop the structure.

The *Castle* looked fully loaded, ready to sail the seas to her next destination.

Clutching his travel bag, Ricardo got off the car, said goodbye to the driver and headed towards the embarcation ladder to the *Castle*. He was now entering a world of steel and moved ahead with the confidence of a seasoned sailor. On reaching the deck, he put down his bag to catch his breath after the steep climb. Casting a glance around he realised he couldn't see anyone in the vicinity. Something was amiss.

As far as he knew, the access was supposed to and ought to be manned at all times. Kicking the board that said 'Show Identification at Gangway,' he started walking towards the office. His instincts seem to guide him in the right direction. He entered a relatively huge room and flung his bag in one corner.

Immediately a man walked in. A thin, short Filipino, he wore tainted orange overalls with retro reflective tape shining on the shoulders, and looked rugged enough for the job.

'Hello friend. I'm Jason, 2nd Mate.'

'Hi. Why isn't there anyone at the gangway?' Ricardo shot back.

'Oh that? Captain sent him to the engine room for some work.'

'Without a replacement?' Ricardo asked raising an eyebrow.

Before Jason could reply, the portable radio on his shoulder came alive with a crackle.

An Indian sounding voice called from the other end, 'Jason, come in.'

'Go ahead,' Ricardo replied without delay.

'Come to my cabin,' the radio crackled.

'Ok sir, coming,' he replied. 'It's the Captain, he's crazy,' Jason told Ricardo and left without waiting for a reply.

Ricardo decided to settle into his new environment, preparing himself mentally and physically for the next encounter when he overheard strange murmurs emerging from the other side of the ship's hospital door, unintentionally left open. That was odd as the outer door to the hospital was always kept locked, more out of concern for law than for sentiments. There was something unusual about the voices on the other side. Someone seemed to be in distress.

Ricardo moved closer to the door and pressed his ear softly to the steel. He couldn't hear anything clearly because of the huge blower howling behind him. He pressed his ear harder against the structure when without warning, something gave him away.

The rusted door opened slightly with an irritating noise, easily overpowering the howl of the blowers. All of a sudden, there was an awkward silence. The murmurs on the other side just disappeared. Ricardo immediately pulled the door open. To his surprise, he saw a tall African, dressed in a white shirt and blue denims, standing all alone in the furnished room.

'Who are you?' Ricardo asked.

The man came out of the room and onto the deck. 'Fred's the name mate. I'm the agent,' he replied sheepishly and started heading towards the gangway.

Before Ricardo could inquire any further, the suspicious-looking man was already on the jetty from where he literally ran out of sight.

Ricardo searched the hospital room but found no one there. He waited for a minute trying to piece together what had just happened. There was nobody at the gangway, he had heard voices in the hospital room and an unidentified African was running all over the ship. He wondered what was going on. As he turned towards the door once again, Jason pulled it open from inside, and stepped out with a short Brazilian man. Both were so engrossed in conversation that Jason didn't see Ricardo standing in front of him, and almost banged into him.

'Now who is he?' Ricardo asked.

'Who, him?' Jason asked, pointing towards his companion. 'Oh! He is Manolo, the agent.'

'What?' Ricardo exclaimed, panic writ across his face. 'Then who was that African who just left?'

'That African?' Jason repeated the words mechanically in his Filipino accent. 'Ok, Ok... listen. I'll go check that out and you, Captain is calling you to his cabin, alright. Straight up last deck.'

With that Jason proceeded to see off the agent.

Ricardo stood still with a blank expression on his face. Was he the only one concerned about the mysterious happenings on the *Castle*? He shot a glance towards the other end of the alleyway as if expecting to see someone. He kept staring at it for a long time but nobody came forth from the emptiness.

~

Ricardo closed the door behind him as he stepped out of the elevator that could only carry three men at a time. 'Captain's Deck,' indicated a board on the door facing the elevator. Ricardo looked around trying to absorb the details of his new world. The alleyway was more like a tunnel, standing six-feet tall and hardly four-feet wide with off-white walls and ceilings. He stopped in front of the second door on the right and read the name out aloud, 'Captain R. Krishnamurthy.' Murthy for short.

'Indian,' he said as he gently knocked on the steel door.

'Come in,' Murthy replied from inside.

Ricardo entered a posh cabin with polished tables in the centre and a large teak sofa in one corner. The floor was richly carpeted and the walls flawless white. The music system on the table was playing a romantic waltz, and Murthy was sitting on an easy chair placed on one side of the room.

'Hello Ricardo, have a seat,' Murthy said as he got up and pushed a teak chair towards Ricardo.

Ricardo sat down in a slow sophisticated manner as if trying to balance a glass on his head. There is a natural respect every sailor has for the Master; he is indeed the king of his terrain—unchallenged, undefeated, omnipotent

When Ricardo finally landed on the seat, he said softly, 'Good evening, Captain.'

'Welcome! We don't have much time, Ricardo. The pilot boards in 20 minutes. We must sail out and head for Esmeraldas, Ecuador. It's a 10-day sail and we must use all the speed we have if we have to make it on time.'

Ricardo listened carefully as the captain brought him up to date on the details of their voyage. The local port navigator was the pilot. He would take the ship out to the open waters before leaving it to the Captain.

Murthy got up and Ricardo followed suit.

'Alright then, I'll be on the bridge. Meet me there in 15 minutes,' Murthy ordered as he started to leave.

'I'll be there, Captain,' Ricardo replied, trying to act as professional as he could, following his first order onboard the *Castle*.

Murthy left the cabin. Ricardo kept staring as the Captain disappeared behind the elevator door. He was alone in the aristocratic room. Even though everything was going smoothly, something was amiss. The air he inhaled felt painfully moist. There was unusual haste and nervousness in the Captain's actions.

In 15 minutes, dressed in a white shirt with two golden bands on the shoulder, and black trousers, Ricardo stood on the bridge, looking every bit an officer and a gentleman. The bridge was the focal centre of the ship, the command house. Ricardo stood in front of a life-size glass wall. From there, crew members running around on the deck looked like ants marching on grass as the green deck extended 180 metres in front of his eyes. It reminded him of the football field in Recife that he turned to for a few hours of escape from the gloom of the orphanage.

Two radar sets ran at the back, their scanners probing the skies for every hidden wonder and obstacle, to project on the big screen on the bridge. The walls were filled with indicators occupying every inch of space available, each showing data that would be Greek to a layman. At the centre was the steering wheel—not a big wooden spring-loaded wheel, but a small automatic control resembling the steering wheel of a Formula 1 car. On each side of the bridge was an open deck marked 'Bridge wings,' to give an even better view of the world they were to sail through.

Two 10,000 horse power tugs pushed the *Castle* from the sea side, holding her along the wharf. Murthy stood on the wing with the pilot. A tall erect Indian, Captain Rajan Krishnamurthy stared into the expanse as if trying to find the answer to an age-old puzzle. Dark skinned with elaborate lines on his forehead, he appeared to be planning strategies all the time. Dressed in fine black [...] white shirt with [...]der, he could have been the [...] an elite force, except he wasn't one. He [...]as the master onboard the *Castle*, a merchant carrier.

Ricardo stood near the engine controls and a seaman stood at the steering wheel looking more focussed than necessary.

On the pilot's advice, the Captain brought the radio to his lips and commanded, 'Let go all lines, forward and aft.'

In an instant, each station responded, 'Roger that, letting go.'

The ropes holding the *Castle* to civilisation slackened into the waters. After 10 minutes of action at the extreme ends, the radio crackled, 'All clear forward.' A little later, another voice crackled, 'All clear aft.'

Murthy looked at Ricardo and for a moment, the lines on Murthy's forehead became more pronounced as sweat rolled down his cheeks. His eyes were shifty and the expression on his face was one of doubt and apprehension. Murthy had taken his decision. As he turned to gaze out of the window, throwing all questions to the sea, he shouted, 'Dead slow ahead.'

In an instant, life returned to normal. Ricardo marked his submission to the Captain, 'Dead slow ahead,' and put the engine control on a DS on the telegraph. Seconds [illegible] A deep rumble emerged from the ke[illegible] the hull, venting the tremor at the bridge. The vibratio[illegible] shook everything on the bridge as the engines tried to put the huge ferrous mass into motion, desperately trying to gather the momentum to literally move a castle. A few minutes on, she started to move.

The tugs started pulling her away from the jetty, kicking up water at the stern. Murthy shouted again, 'Half ahead.' Ricardo complied.

A deeper tremor hit the *Castle* increasing her pace in the blue. After 15 minutes of manoeuvring, she was clear of the land that she had recently been tethered to.

The pilot picked up his bag, ready to leave as his boat found it hard to keep up with the increasing speed of the big carrier.

Murthy and Ricardo stood alone on the bridge. Neither of them spoke; both kept staring at the vast ocean while the sun shone on the deck, stirring up their thoughts. Each one was trying to seek an answer to what destiny would bring their way in the coming days. It was a voyage both had waited for longer than they could remember.

Finally, Murthy turned towards Ricardo and both of them stared at each other. The expression on their face hardened as each tried to guess what was going on in the other's mind.

The *Castle* had commenced her voyage for Ecuador.

She had been out sailing for almost a day now and there was no sign of land. The swell had picked up and the sea could be seen moving up almost four metres from its rest. The *Castle* was riding the crests and troughs regally, commanding the waters beneath, engaging with every wave streaming by.

Ricardo stood in uniform on the bridge next to the chart, staring at the small islands next to Jamaica—The Windward Isles. He was in an imaginary world, breathing life into the dull chart, drawing a world he always wanted to be in. He saw endless glassy waters, coloured green by the corals on the shallow seabed with rare patches of blue. A lighthouse shone in the distance, like the Pole Star, proud of its radiance. The wind whispered siren songs in his ears. Slowly the sun came out from behind the clouds and directed its beams at the waters beneath. Ricardo smiled as the rays touched his face and bathed the world around him in a supernatural glow. The dull chart was finally breathing. His dreamland was almost within reach.

The sharp ring of the elevator's arrival alarm made Ricardo snap back to the bridge. He looked towards the clock as it struck nine in the morning.

Captain Murthy stepped out of the elevator with the chief officer, Korpovich, a Russian of average height with a small beer belly. His light hair and complexion made him appear all the more pale next to the swarthy Captain. Ricardo had already met him in the morning at breakfast.

Murthy was in uniform and his walk complemented the appeal. He strode towards the communication panel determinedly. Ricardo kept his eyes on the Captain till he returned the gaze. Murthy stopped in front of a white handset lying on a small table. The label read, 'INMARSAT PHONE'. Without warning, he pulled out the phone wire and started wrapping up the set in plastic foil.

Ricardo walked up to him and quietly stood on the side of the table without taking his eyes off the target.

'Everything alright, Captain?' he asked casually.

'There will be no phone facility for a few days,' Murthy replied hastily as though he had already prepared the answer.

'That's what I thought,' Ricardo nodded calmly.

Murthy finished wrapping the handset and put it in a locker in the corner. 'The satellite subscription expired yesterday. I have sent a notice for renewal. Till then, the phone cannot be used. Is that clear?'

'Absolutely, sir.' Ricardo knew, onboard, the Captain's word was final.

~

Stories flew thick and furious about Murthy's personal life. According to rumours at the dining table, Murthy had underplayed his part as a husband and his significant other had filed for a divorce a month ago. He had heated arguments with her over the phone to which most officers had become unwilling witnesses.

After the news of Murthy's divorce had spread, when Korpovich had expressed his concern over the matter, Murthy had taken offence.

While everyone was on the bridge wing to take in the cool ocean breeze, Korpovich asked the Captain hesitantly, 'If anyone wants to call home, what should we say?'

Murthy did not look at Korpovich. With his eyes fixed on the waters, he took a deep breath of the untainted air. 'It'll all be over in a few days,' he whispered, as if to himself.

Ricardo, who was leaning against the railing, looked at Murthy quizzically, 'Excuse me sir, but I did not hear that?'

Murthy tore his gaze away from the ocean and looked at Ricardo. Beneath the calm lurked a nebulous fear. 'The satellite will be fine in a few days. Everyone can call their families after that.' Murthy left the wing to avoid further questions.

Korpovich seemed a little lost. Of late, Murthy had been behaving oddly but Korpovich put that down to the divorce.

Ricardo stood unmoved at the edge of the railing, looking at the waters rise and fall to their own unique rhythm. Then he shut his eyes and said to the ocean, 'It'll all be over in a few days.'

Time, the great ally that Ricardo and Murthy counted on to lead them to freedom, was in reality propelling them to an end neither could foresee.

~

As the clock struck six, dinner was served onboard the *Castle*. Ricardo sat alone at a six seat table as the steward served king prawns cooked in thick spicy sauce, garnished with olives. He was about to take his first bite when Jason walked into the mess singing loudly in Tagalog, his native language.

'Ricardo!' he shouted. 'Life is good my friend.'

'What's up?' Ricardo asked calmly.

'As they say, no news is good news,' he replied with a smile.

'And what exactly is the "no news" today?' Ricardo enquired.

'Well, Captain says no noon reports to be sent till the satellite thing is ok. That means almost no work.'

Going by what the noon reports were, Jason's glee was justified.

Over half a dozen parties are involved in making a ship sail smoothly across the seas. It starts with a person somewhere on the planet, who spends his money to buy a vessel, so he becomes an owner. But he doesn't know much about the seas and owns a vessel, so he lends her on charter to a second party called charterer.

The charterer arranges for what the ship carries and to which destination, drawing up a simple contract with the owner on what could be called, a rental scheme. Now the charterer doesn't have anything to transport, so he gets hold of a third party, the shipper.

The shipper actually owns the cargo travelling by sea, and pays freight for moving their cargo from one place to the other, and finally to the charterer. The shipper's counterpart is the receiver who waits for his cargo at the destination port rather impatiently. It was all pretty simple till here. Now there is a ship and the cargo, but no one to manage either. This is when the management comes into the picture.

The management takes care of the manning and regulation compliances of a ship. To complicate matters, the owner chooses the management.

Since large amounts of money are involved in the transactions, an insurance company is involved. The ship and cargo are insured by the owner. And as the vessel sails further, other establishments come into the picture trying to make a buck here and there, every now and then.

Jason was to send a daily noon report of the *Castle* to almost all of them.

'Phones will start ringing all over if you don't send the reports. You know the formalities,' Ricardo insisted.

'Ah, old man says he'll take care of them,' Jason replied nonchalantly.

'And how does he intend to do that?'

Ricardo's final question set Jason thinking. For a minute, he tried to figure out a sensible answer and then gave up, 'Let him think of that. You, my friend, are unnecessarily tense. Have a beer, you'll feel better.' He winked as he left the room singing the same Tagalog song.

Ricardo stared into the bowl on the table, trying to make sense of what was happening. All of a sudden, the dead prawns lying in the pool of red sauce ignited his imagination. The red sauce turned into deep waters and all that was dead in the sauce sprung back to life. The prawns were participating in a parade, all of them with faces of people Ricardo had met over the past few days. He found himself climbing a huge wave. As he reached the crest, he saw more familiar faces gathered around a big prawn who had Murthy's face. 'The King Prawn,' Ricardo thought.

The king held his spectre high with his arms outstretched, apparently trying to gather more than he could manage. He smiled smugly as the voices hailing him in an alien tongue grew louder. Ricardo saw another prawn poised in a dark corner, his face concealed by the shadows. His crusty exterior shone menacingly in the dark. As the prawn raised his swimmerets towards the king, Ricardo noticed a gun in one of them. The dark entity let out a horrifying laugh as he pressed the trigger, shaking Ricardo to his core.

The deafening sound of the gunshot blocked off every other sound before the world began swirling before Ricardo's eyes.

A sudden gust of wind brought Ricardo back to the dinner table. He looked at the Captain's chair. With a faint smile on his lips he said to himself, 'Play ball!'

~

It was a dark night. The moon had been consumed by clouds claiming the skies with their overwhelming black. The air was humid after a long day of rains. Ricardo stood in front of the compass on the bridge, concentrating on the emptiness which lay ahead. A lookout in orange overalls stood lazily in one corner with his weight resting against the auto-pilot stand. Ricardo focused on the course of the *Castle*, monitoring every manoeuvre, keeping it in safe waters. Behind him, the chart room had been covered on all sides with thick curtains to trap all light within the navigation centre.

Ricardo went into the chart room to plot a position as the clock struck nine. He had always been amused by the strange comparison of a chart room with a prison cell. The 'prison cell,' a metaphor of darkness, had actually been lit up while the world outside, presumably clean, pure, enlightened, was darker than the night. But wasn't that the frightening truth of the new world order? So on which side was Ricardo playing?

He finished fixing the position on the chart and walked back into the dark, repositioning himself in front of the compass for a review of the seas around. He was about to say something to the lookout when the phone rang, tearing asunder the silence of the night.

Ignoring the unusual timing of the call, Ricardo reached for the phone. 'Bridge, Ricardo here,' he said in a memorised accent.

A frightened Jason stammered at the other end, 'Ricardo, there is somebody here. A ghost… help!'

'Calm down, Jason,' Ricardo said reassuringly.

Jason did not respond.

His authoritative tone did not help. 'Where are you, Jason?' he asked calmly.

'Provision… provision store,' Jason stammered, trying to fight his fears.

'Just stay there. I'm sending the lookout to you. He'll bring you up to the bridge.'

He disconnected and turned to an alert lookout.

'Jason is in the provision store. Just assist him up to the bridge. I'll call the Captain,' Ricardo said as he turned towards the phone to make a call. The lookout was about to leave the bridge when Ricardo turned and said, 'And make sure neither of you talk to anybody on your way up.' From the expression on Ricardo's face, the lookout understood that he meant business, and left the deck, closing the door quietly behind him.

~

It was an unusually dark night. Jason stood on the bridge surrounded by Murthy, Korpovich, Ricardo and the lookout. He was trembling with fright and felt grateful for the human wall shielding him.

Ricardo narrated the whole story to the Captain who was dressed in what seemed to be a night suit. As he finished, he added, 'It could be a stowaway?'

'What nonsense!' shouted a livid Murthy, summarily dismissing the suggestion. 'You think it's a joke? A stowaway! And that too from Brazil to Ecuador!'

'Captain, a search of the provision store wouldn't harm anyone,' replied Ricardo, as calmly as he had narrated the whole situation.

Before Murthy could launch on a tirade, Korpovich tipped the scales in Ricardo's favour. 'I agree with him. A search should be alright.'

Murthy was clearly uneasy. He looked for an excuse to override Ricardo and Korpovich's suggestion, and was about to speak when Ricardo interrupted him, 'Captain, I insist!'

Fifteen minutes after the exchange on the bridge, a search party assembled in the galley, in front of the provision store. Murthy, Korpovich and Ricardo stood next to a life-size oven, its chrome plating shining in the bright lamp overhead. Each one held a big search light with 'Wolf' written in bold letters on it.

Jason was left on the bridge to recover from the trauma of having encountered a ghost. The lookout was told to stay back with him for the much-needed moral support.

Three brave men in the galley stared quietly at the door marked 'Provision Store', each one trying to mask his fears: 'What if it is actually a stowaway?' 'What if he is armed?' 'What if there are more than one?'

Murthy moved forward and tugged at the door that swung open noiselessly. As he let go of the knob, the door swung back, banging the steel bulkhead with its heavy might. The ear-shattering sound jangled everyone's nerves. It took a while for the sound to die out.

Korpovich let out a laugh. 'F*****g grease!' he said in his hard Russian accent, making it sound more like a joke than a complaint.

They entered a small room with doors on all three sides, labelled Dry Provision, Fish Room and Cold Storage. The first two were sealed with small brass locks, the keys kept safely in the cook's cabin. But the lock for the Cold Storage was missing. It was surely a stowaway because if anyone was indeed hiding onboard the *Castle*, he would need food sooner rather than later.

Korpovich picked up a small broomstick lying next to the main door, and held it like a sword, bracing himself for an attack.

'And what exactly do you plan to do with that?' Ricardo asked.

Korpovich didn't reply. Perhaps the broomstick was a stupid idea after all.

Suddenly Murthy stepped forward and slowly opened the Cold Storage door. An awfully cold misty air rushed out into the warmer, smaller room. Or was it fear chilling their senses? To add to their misery, the lights suddenly went out. There was no separate switch for the small room. All rooms in the Provision Store were fed by the main switchboard.

The search party switched on their torches as they fought to keep fear at bay. The powerful beams shot across the room casting large halos on the surrounding walls. Moving in close-knit formation, they waited at the door for their eyes to get used to the dark.

As they stepped inside, their breathing became laboured. White misty vapour emanated from their mouths and nostrils. The store was a long room divided into three sections by single-piece steel shelves which had been stacked to the top with cold foods for the long voyage ahead. Murthy signalled his two associates to split up and search each section individually. They proceeded to their assigned sections to look for any abnormality. In the deathly silence, each step they took could be heard across the length and breadth of the store. Ricardo held the torch with both hands as though it were a pistol. He recalled a game he had played in his childhood. Every senseless toy was a weapon with which he had always shot down imaginative beasts. He kept checking all corners. Just as he reached one end of his section, he heard a muffled cry from the other end.

'Who is it?' he shouted without thinking of the impact.

To his relief, Murthy replied from the other corner, 'Nobody, just me. It's clear.'

Immediately Korpovich hollered from his section, 'Same here, not even a rat.'

Ricardo quickly glanced at the two dark corners and shouted, 'Well then, what are we waiting for? Let's get out of here.'

They all gathered outside their sections. The search had yielded nothing.

'Satisfied?' Murthy said spitefully to Ricardo. 'You should think twice before making such suggestions.'

The entrance door to the Provision Store was firmly shut and the three doors inside were well secured too.

After a few minutes of silence, the knob of the main door slowly turned and the door creaked open.

~

It was yet another bright and sunny day onboard the *Castle*. Murthy had instructed the search party to not utter a word to anyone about the previous night. 'I don't want any unnecessary speculations.' But sound travels faster through metal.

At breakfast, everyone was talking about it. The story had been generously spiced up. By the time breakfast was over, two groups were arguing bitterly. Some thought that there was indeed a stowaway on board while others believed it could have been a ghost. A third group believed that the whole story had been cooked up for entertainment, and a fourth group couldn't care less.

Having a stowaway on board was a matter of serious concern. The vessel was required by law to serve stowaways proper food, provide them with living quarters and not subject them to physical work. Due to such laws, stowaways normally turned themselves in after the vessel was out of their country's limits. At times, when a vessel reached a destination, the authorities would simply refuse to accept the unwanted stowaways.

'We do not have permission to disembark them yet,' was the usual reply of immigration officers at most ports. The Captain would keep fighting till the vessel sailed out, with the troublemakers still on board. This way they became the property and responsibility of the vessel till a generous country agreed to accept them, or till they were deported to their country of origin.

Murthy remained quiet at the table. He chose to ignore the conflicting versions of the previous night's happenings that were doing the rounds. Already cut up about the disrupted satellite telephone service, the crew now had another story to carry back home. But when were the phone services likely to be restored? Galley rumours had it that the Captain had been using the phone from his cabin, but most of it was speculation.

All this while, the *Castle* kept shrugging off waves as it continued to slither on the ocean's surface. It had covered a significant distance since its last port. Churning the waters, the *Castle* was almost past the northern edge of South American land and now fast approaching the Caribbean islands.

In the blinding darkness, the waters beneath could only be felt from the thrust of the *Castle*. The sky was overridden with soft nimbus clouds. By moonlight, the horizon appeared to be within reach.

~

Ricardo stood on the edge of the port bridge wing, feeling the breeze against his hair, his body, his uniform. Positioning himself on the ledge with his weight on the railing, he rested his arms on the bulwark. As he stared into the dark ocean, he thought of himself as a king standing in front of his subjects hailing his greatness as they bowed to him. Many thoughts cluttered his head. He seemed to be in a maze, invariably ending up at the start just when he was sure of having gotten out of it.

He thought of his past deeds, good, bad and ugly, but was even more concerned about what he had yet to do. Life was more complicated than it had seemed in the beginning. The complications though had mostly been personal. Ricardo had always positioned himself as a contender for a seat in heaven, but recent developments were forcing him to take a reality check. 'There's nothing wrong in this. In fact, this might have been the only right thing to do!' he kept convincing himself.

The chronograph on his wrist beeped as it struck nine. Ricardo was about to begin another attempt to get through the maze when he heard footsteps right behind him. Swinging back in haste, he was more shocked than surprised to see the intruder, but before he could turn around completely, the intruder pushed him over the edge with all his might.

A helpless Ricardo struggled hard for a foothold but finally gave in, slipping off the bridge wing as he saw his body falling almost 30 metres vertically into the ocean beneath. He kept trying to catch the thin air with his fist in an attempt to save himself. Anybody falling overboard, unnoticed at night, on the high seas, could unmistakably be written off as a life lost. He let out a loud scream. The roaring ocean mercilessly stifled it. He was falling to his death. As he neared the ocean's surface, he looked up at the wing trying to discern his murderer. Someone stood at the place where he had stood a few seconds ago. The man wore a black long coat with a hood pulled over his face. His bloodshot eyes shone frighteningly in the dark. The ghostly figure was the demon Ricardo had seen in his nightmares. Clearly the grim reaper.

As the questions on the dying man's mind turned into fear—the fear of what lay beyond death—time froze, with Ricardo suspended midair a few centimetres above water. The incessant roar of the ocean stopped, and the waters made way to receive him as he made his last descent towards nothingness. A strong wind suddenly lifted the hood on the murderer's receding head. Captain Murthy leaned over the edge with a smile on his lips. Ricardo closed his eyes to shut out the horror as his body met the waters in a bone-crushing splash.

Ricardo woke up in his cabin sweating profusely. It took him almost a minute to realise that he had had a nightmare. Throwing off the blanket, he dragged himself out of bed, still weighed down by what he had just seen. Surely it wasn't just a nightmare; surely it portended something.

He walked into the bathroom and turned on the tap. Chilled water gushed forth. Ricardo filled his palms with the cold relief and splashed it on his face, washing away sweat, and with it, the confusion. Turning off the tap, he looked at the mirror. An alien stared back at him. He looked intensely at his own reflection, trying to figure out his present. As he felt the answers coming to him, he understood what the encounter in the other world meant. And he told himself, 'I can't do this.'

4

Tro's Kingdom

At his fortified mansion, Tro sat lazily in his cushioned sunbathing chair. The beige of the cushion offset his black gown—Tro stood out in his surroundings. Armed guards went about their regular routine.

Tro mulled over what lay ahead. He had thought through each detail to make it the perfect plan. He wasn't nervous. He had masterminded too many crimes across the world to be lily-livered now. His real name, like his innocent self, had been lost with time. Tro was his absolute identity now.

The master-plotter was half asleep when his phone rang. Almost on cue, the guards took position. Tro reached for the set tucked into the front pocket of his robe. The screen flashed 'Unknown', which was hardly unusual as most of his associates preferred to keep their identity a secret. He thought it was one of his companions, but to his surprise, the voice on the other side wasn't a familiar one.

A woman spoke briskly in a neat Japanese accent, 'Good Morning Mr Tro, this is Yoko from the Yakuza. I have some urgent matters to discuss with you regarding the bid for the data.'

'I'm sorry Miss Yoko,' he responded sharply, 'The deal is already closed. There is no further scope for negotiations.'

'I am not trying to negotiate with you,' she replied calmly, before adding, 'I wish to warn you about the intentions of the Chinese. They can never be trusted. The General is setting a trap for you.'

'Hold on Miss Yoko,' Tro interrupted her. 'And what exactly is your interest in this?'

'That is immaterial,' she continued. 'I am your well-wisher. The General wishes to retire after this deal is through. To have an honorable retirement, he will compromise you. The money of course shall not be declared to anyone, and he will be untraceable after he is through. He must have asked you for delivery to China?'

Tro heard her out. 'And how do you know all this?'

'We have our sources. Let me explain our interest in all this. We will help you get out of this conspiracy safely after the deal is made. In return, the data comes to us. The Chinese money is yours along with an additional payment from us and a token of our friendship. What we gain is nobody's business.' She paused and then added, 'What do you say?'

There was an uneasy silence at both ends. Tro tried to figure out what Yoko's offer was all about. But before he could say anything, she spoke again. 'Time is of the essence Tro. If you intend to work with us, you must decide now. This is for your own good.'

Tro's mind was racing, 'What's the plan?'

Yoko discussed everything that could go wrong and right. There was no room for any more surprises.

~

As soon as he stepped into his plush limousine, Tro pulled out his cell phone and punched in a number he had memorised. 'Hello darling. There's been a slight change of plans. The caretaker seems to be double dealing. He's going to need substantial motivation from your end.'

He waited for an update from the other side and then said, 'Yes, let's go with Plan B. Keep me informed.'

He didn't want to do this but difficult times called for grave measures.

5

Adrift on the Atlantic

Ricardo was fighting his demons. It was a bright afternoon and he sat in his cabin on a black leather upholstered chair, leaning towards the centre table which had a small marble chessboard. His white overall had his name tag just above the chest, held in place by a small piece of Velcro. The game had started; warriors from both camps had already made their initial moves.

He was totally immersed in the black and white war when the *Castle* suddenly sprang back to life with a familiar roar. Within seconds, the piercing fire alarm shook life on board. Ricardo glanced at the fire bell above his bed trying to cope up with the disturbing decibel. Thirty seconds later, Korpovich informed everyone through the PA system, 'Fire in engine room, I repeat, fire in engine room. All crew muster. Emergency stations!'

coloured deck, all attention turned to him. The second stowaway who had his back to Ricardo spun around with appreciable speed. Whipping out a small pistol, he took aim at Ricardo's head. To Ricardo's surprise, it was a girl. Her perfect silhouette came through the skin-tight black trousers and shirt that she wore. Her short spiky hair covered her ears. Sharp featured, she cut a contrast with Murthy, now a hostage. Her partner in crime called out to her. Her name was Daze.

Ricardo looked straight into her light brown eyes and, for a second, forgot about the gun in her hand. Murthy was struggling desperately in the other stowaway's arms. Dressed in blue denims and a white T-shirt, he looked Latino. He shouted something in Spanish, clearly asking Ricardo to stay put or else Murthy would pay the price.

'Back off,' Daze shouted to Ricardo in a clean English accent, pointing the gun to his head .

'Alright, I'm not doing anything,' Ricardo replied cautiously.

In the scuffle which had taken place before Ricardo arrived, Murthy had been overpowered in no time. His nose was bleeding profusely and there was a gash across his left eyebrow.

'What do you want?' said Ricardo trying to negotiate Murthy's release.

'Hands behind your head,' hissed Daze.

Instead, Ricardo started walking towards Murthy in slow calculated steps. The Latino killer shouted hysterically as he saw Ricardo approach. Ricardo noticed a small pistol lying on the deck. In the scuffle between Murthy and the Latino, it had landed there.

Now Ricardo stood dangerously close to the gleaming object. Suddenly the Latino looked as scared as Murthy. Daze made no move to stop Ricardo who said to the Latino in a calm slow voice, 'Let him go and we'll talk.'

The Latino let out a loud cry as he pushed Murthy towards him.

Ricardo ducked to avoid colliding with Murthy who landed on the deck right next to the pistol. In a jiffy, Murthy grabbed the weapon and aimed it at the Latino who rushed towards his partner in crime and snatched the gun from her hands. Ricardo tried to move out of range but was caught between the killer and Murthy, both on the verge of exchanging gunfire. The man pointed the gun at Murthy's head, shouting in Spanish as he charged forward. Looking straight into Murthy's eyes, he pulled the trigger. A small clicking sound emanated from the gun. It had no bullet.

Murthy did not wait for a second attempt on his life and pressed the trigger. The loud bang was followed by an uneasy silence. The bullet grazed Ricardo's arm and made a hole on the stowaway's right shoulder. Blood dyed the injured man's white shirt red. He dragged himself towards the shipside railing and without any attempt to save himself, fell overboard crashing into the hungry waters beneath.

Ricardo and Daze watched in stunned silence. A paralysed Murthy dropped the gun to the deck and stared at his hands in disbelief. Ricardo moved swiftly, picked up the gun and aimed it at Daze. Hands behind her head, she had little choice but to surrender.

'I didn't do it. I didn't kill him, Ricardo. He was going to shoot me. You saw him press the trigger, didn't you? I didn't kill anyone Ricardo,' pleaded Murthy, as though Ricardo were a federal judge.

'Listen to me Captain, look at me,' Ricardo was shaking Murthy. 'Nobody saw you fire that gun except the two of us, right. Nobody knows there were two of them. So let's lock her up first, then we'll think of what to do,' he reassured Murthy.

'And she certainly wouldn't say anything, would you?' Murthy looked straight into Daze's eyes. If they could kill one, they could kill another.

Daze quietly turned herself in as hostage. Ricardo asked her to surrender other concealed weapons.

'Are there any more of you?'

'No.'

'You better be sure of that. I won't mind getting rid of you if you try any stunts. Are we clear?'

'Yes,' she replied.

'Good, now help me pick him up.'

They were about to leave when Ricardo heard a movement from across the bridge. He needed to check that. To his relief, there was nothing. Images of the bloodbath he had just witnessed swam in his head. Daze and he lifted a visibly traumatised Murthy and took him to his cabin before summoning a medical officer.

Locked up in a small room on board the *Castle*, Daze reflected on life's twists and turns. She was desperate to hold a gun again.

~

Murthy put the event behind him. As Captain, that was expected of him. Dressed in a polo shirt and plain brown trousers, he relaxed in his cabin. Ricardo had not seen him since their last action-packed meeting.

There was one captured stowaway on board. That was the official story. No one spoke about the stowaway adrift on the ocean. Was he dead or still alive?

Concerned about Murthy's well-being, Ricardo decided to pay him a visit.

Still in uniform after completing his watch, Ricardo headed towards Murthy's cabin. Barely had he reached the steel entrance and was about to knock, he stopped. He could hear muffled voices inside. He pressed his ear to the door. Murthy was speaking gruffly to someone, but Ricardo couldn't hear the interlocutor. Maybe he was at the farther end of the cabin.

Curious to see who Murthy was talking to, Ricardo swung open the steel door in a single swift motion. To his surprise, Murthy stood alone next to his study. There was nobody else in that room. But Ricardo was sure he had heard Murthy talk to someone. Surely he wasn't talking to himself.

Then the pieces of the puzzle came together. Murthy's left hand was still on the satellite phone.

'What are you trying to do, young man?' Murthy yelled, clearly agitated. 'Haven't you heard of knocking before you enter?'

Ricardo didn't listen to what Murthy said. His eyes travelled to the satellite handset. 'The phone is working?'

'Ricardo!' Murthy shouted back. 'Go to the bridge. I'll see everyone there in 15 minutes.'

Ricardo stepped back from the door and stood still, staring at Murthy.

'Now!' barked Murthy.

Ricardo turned back immediately and headed towards the exit. He turned to see what Murthy was doing but he saw an empty room. Murthy had disappeared.

'So much for saving your life, Captain,' he muttered to himself as he entered the elevator and pressed the button.

The crew, mostly in stained overalls, gathered on the bridge wondering why they had been summoned. The door to the bridge opened with a light click. All heads turned towards it, expecting to see their Captain who had captured a stowaway the previous evening. Instead, Korpovich walked in, rubbing his eyes. He walked up to Jason and whispered in his ear, 'Old man's here?'

'Not yet,' nodded Jason.

'What does he want now?' asked Korpovich loudly.

'He said he'll be here in 15 minutes,' Ricardo confirmed.

In another minute the door opened again. Murthy entered in uniform, holding a bunch of papers in his hand. He looked stern. The lines on his forehead seemed to have deepened.

He went straight to the chart table in the centre and everyone gathered around him. Korpovich looked at Murthy and said, 'Captain, don't you think it's a little crowded in here? You mind if we go on the wing?'

'No. It's better here,' he replied hastily, wiping his sweating face with a handkerchief. Resting his weight on the chart table, he took a deep breath and started the speech he had been long preparing. 'Gentlemen, as you all know, yesterday, we had rather intriguing events onboard. We now have a stowaway with us, detained in the cable store for now. Thankfully, there were no casualties.'

Murthy paused for a while. He shut his eyes for a moment to clear his thoughts. 'Now, let me explain why you all have been called here.' Looking pointedly at Ricardo, he said aloud, 'Firstly, the satellite phone has been activated and we are receiving voice and data but outgoing transfers are still barred.'

Ricardo didn't react to the news.

Murthy looked at the crew who seemed pleased at the news. Then he said, 'I've had a word with the owners and informed them about the whole incident. They have decided to divert the vessel and carry out a detailed investigation into the matter. The case has turned legal now and is totally out of my hands.

'The vessel will be handed over to the authorities at Curaçao. You all shall be repatriated to your home towns from there. We will be reaching Curaçao tomorrow morning.'

The crew looked tense. Murthy waited for the news to settle in and said with a reassuring smile, 'What are you waiting for people? Start packing!'

His words brought back a smile on everyone's face. The crew started exiting the bridge, chatting animatedly, already exchanging goodbyes. Strangely, when they were home, they wished to join the vessel and when on board, they invariably wished to be back home.

Murthy signalled his officers to stay back. Jason, Korpovich and Ricardo stood next to the chart table.

Murthy made himself a cup of black coffee and holding the mug close to his lips, he said, 'As you all might have heard, Curaçao is an island north of Trinidad.'

Curaçao was a moderate-sized island in the Caribbean region north of South American mainland. Though the island was scarcely bigger than a state, it was an independent country, a part of the Netherlands Antilles. It had been taking in sea-going vessels and, over time, had turned into a much-sought-after destination, tourist and commercial.

Murthy pulled out a chart from under the table and spread it out. The chart was a detailed description of the regions around the small island they were diverted to. Ricardo looked at the harbour entrance of Curaçao and without taking his sight off the document, thought out loud, 'Willemstad, that's the harbour, I suppose, on the western side.' He sought a confirmation.

'Yes it is, Ricardo,' Murthy replied softly. 'But we will be approaching on the eastern end.' He ran his finger along the chart as he continued explaining their passage through the small islands covering the vast oceans which lay untouched around the area. 'We shall approach from the north of this island, Klein Curaçao,' he pointed to a small isolated yellow patch just south of the main island. 'We'll pass the 1000-metre contour and approach the southern mouth here,' he continued, pointing to coordinates on the chart. 'We have been instructed to stop and drift in that region and wait for further instructions. Any questions?'

'Do we need to make any report, notice or anything?' Jason asked casually, subconsciously calculating the answer.

'That won't be necessary,' Murthy replied. 'Well then, that's settled, you all can go and pack.'

'It's a bit surprising how fast it's all happening,' Korpovich chipped in.

'Well I can't really say anything about that, can I?' Murthy seemed reluctant to address the officer's query.

'And what about the stowaway?' Korpovich persisted.

'She'll be handed over to the authorities here. You'll see what happens when we reach, Korpovich. Now if you'll please excuse me, I have some documents to prepare,' replied Murthy, snuffing out further conversation. Then he exited the bridge abruptly.

6

Somewhere off Curaçao

As the *Castle* headed out of the deep churning into the shallows of the Caribbean islands, Murthy stood erect on the bridge wearing his usual formal attire. He had been up all night. He stared at the life-size glass windows that lined the front peer of the bridge. His eyes were locked on the horizon as night was laid to rest by the first ray of the sun that fanned out in the skies. The calm waters merged into the serene surroundings slowly coming to life. The breeze seemed to get colder and the heat of the sun reminded him of the Arctic and the Tropics at the same time. The waters turned crystal clear as the ocean bed stirred with shoals of sprinting fish. Murthy shut his eyes, reliving every second of his life as Captain on board the *Castle*. The sound of the rising waters had the power to banish all pain and confusion.

Working on the chart table, preparing to make landfall, Jason interrupted Murthy's cogitations. 'Captain, Klein Curaçao is in sight, two points on the port bow.'

Murthy opened his eyes and looked straight at the sun, now three quarters above the horizon, looking like a massive ball of fire, shrinking slowly as it rose. He brought himself back to the bridge. Holding up a pair of black Nikon binoculars to his eyes, he peered at the right direction. 'Good, keep steering on this course till we reach the 1000-metre contour.'

'Aye, aye, Captain,' Jason said boldly.

The *Castle* inched forward towards its destination with a helmsman on the wheel keeping the vessel where it ought to be. Slowly, the tiny island in the distance grew closer and bigger. On the eastern edge of the island stood a small lighthouse. Behind the island lay a much larger landmass. That was where they were heading, their final destination, the island of Curaçao.

'Hitting the 1000 mark now, Captain,' Jason said.

Murthy looked at Jason, 'Bring her to half ahead.'

'Half ahead,' Jason replied to the orders and adjusted the engine telegraph.

The *Castle* slowed down as it got closer to the growing landmass, running on her own momentum. They were about to make landfall near the deserted eastern edge of the small island.

'We're approaching the southern mouth, Captain,' said Jason as he came out of the chart room looking confused. 'You're sure this is it? I can't see anybody here.'

'Stop engines,' Murthy said, ignoring Jason.

'Yes Captain,' Jason replied sheepishly as he brought the *Castle* to a stop.

'They'll be here any minute now. We drift and wait,' Murthy said calmly.

'Yes Captain,' Jason replied with a faint smile.

As the *Castle* drifted to a halt, floating in the territorial waters of Curaçao, Korpovich and Ricardo entered the bridge dressed in casuals—faded blue denims and T-shirts.

'We're already there?' Ricardo asked Jason.

'Yeah, Cap says this is it,' Jason replied indifferently.

'Korpovich!' Murthy called out.

'Yes, Captain?' Korpovich replied looking straight at Murthy.

'Have you mustered everyone like I told you?' Murthy asked softly, in probably their last minutes together.

Murthy had asked Korpovich to gather all crew in the smoke room with their luggage, saying that it was a requirement of the port authorities. They were to leave from there itself.

'Yes Captain, they are all gathered and ready to go and the girl is in the office,' Korpovich replied cheerfully.

Suddenly the VHF set mounted on the front end of the bridge crackled to life, 'Motor Vessel *Castle*, Motor Vessel *Castle*, this is your agent speaking. Come in please.' The voice was crude with a rustic accent.

Murthy immediately rushed to the set. 'Yes agent, this is *Castle* replying. Captain speaking.'

'Good morning Captain, welcome to Curaçao.'

Everyone on the bridge let out a small laugh as the Captain replied to the gesture, 'Yes, thank you. What's the plan?' Murthy got straight to the point.

'Alright Captain, is everyone ready to leave? I am bringing the signing-off boat with me.'

'Yes, everything is ready. When are you coming?'

'I am on my way. Please lower your gangway.'

Everyone went out to the bridge wing, anticipating the agent. To their surprise, five white high-speed boats headed towards the *Castle,* leaving a trail of froth that swiftly spread across the ocean as it raced to meet the horizon.

Three of the boats had 'POLICE' painted in black on both sides in large letters. The other two were unmarked and relatively less occupied. The constabulary boats spread out as they approached and started to circle the vessel, their outboard engines roaring with every spin and strain.

Murthy and his officers stood on the deck looking at the two boats approaching the gangway. One of the boats had two men dressed in formal brown suits, each holding a similar black briefcase. Their attire seemed more like a uniform.

Murthy and Ricardo walked up to the boarding personnel as they stepped onto the main deck. They took out their identity cards and held them up to their receivers.

'Hello Captain, I am Caster, the agent,' one of the men spoke looking straight at Murthy. He seemed to be in his late twenties and was well built, with a pleasing face and smile. His tanned skin and thick black hair made him look rather formal.

'You want me to frisk them?' Ricardo asked Murthy.

'That won't be necessary, Ricardo,' replied Murthy.

'Hello, you came with friends,' Murthy asked the agent, pointing at the federal boats which were still circling the vessel probably carrying out their customary search.

'Not my choice, Captain,' the agent replied with an ironic smile, shrugging his shoulders as he spoke. 'Well Captain, we don't have much time here. This is my associate, Matt. He will take the crew off for you.'

'Ok and when will that be?' Murthy inquired.

'Now, Captain,' the agent replied promptly. 'Where is the girl?'

'She is in the office. We have sedated her to avoid unnecessary trouble,' Murthy replied, a bit perturbed.

'We must take a look Captain, just you and me,' the agent spoke bluntly, indicating that the officers were to stay behind.

Murthy quietly led the agent to his cabin.

In 20 minutes, the crew had boarded the boat intended to take them ashore. Murthy handed over their passports to Matt. When everyone seemed settled in the boat, Korpovich and Ricardo walked up to Murthy standing next to the main deck exit with the agent. He was unusually silent as he moved along the railings looking at the crew.

Ricardo walked up to him, 'Everyone aboard, Captain. Do you want me to fetch your bags?'

'What? Umm, no. No thank you Ricardo, that won't be necessary.'

'What do you mean?' Korpovich barged in.

'I'm staying back a little longer. Have some formalities to complete here, and the stowaway to hand over,' Murthy's reply seemed rehearsed.

Korpovich sensed the unease in Murthy's voice, 'Captain, it's a saying back home that we must be careful when something goes too wrong or too right. Think about that.'

Ricardo looked at the old man. He seemed restless.

'I'll be alright. You boys carry on. It was nice sailing with you all. Maybe we'll meet again,' he said with a forced smile.

'I have a feeling that we will, Captain,' Ricardo said, still looking into Murthy's eyes.

Everyone disembarked the *Castle* and got onto the boat which was still burning fuel alongside the gangway. The federal boats with armed guards had stopped their interrogation and were quietly floating around with their engines killed.

Then the boat pulled away taking the crew of the *Castle* with it. As it slowly sped away, the *Castle* grew smaller.

Ricardo looked out of the window at the receding deck where they had left Murthy. He was still there, standing alone. Even from that distance, Murthy looked uncertain. Soon the *Castle* disappeared from sight. It was then that Ricardo sensed something was not right.

The crew was sitting on wooden benches along the periphery of the boat. Nobody else seemed to care about leaving the Captain behind except Korpovich and Ricardo. Deep down Ricardo knew that Murthy had played his hand. Ricardo's mind wondered back to a few days ago. How neatly they had blanked out the story of the second stowaway to save Murthy, or was he barking up the wrong tree?

Ricardo looked at the chronograph on his wrist. It was five past nine. He remembered the old man on the sidewalk he had met back home. He was trying to presage something. What?

The boat kept churning up a mini cyclone as it pulled further away from the *Castle* and moved towards the mainland. After steaming for 20 minutes, a sudden calm hit the waters. The seas looked like a glass surface swaying to nature's melody. The air was still. The only noise was of the powerful outboard engine. Slowly the skies became overrun with thick clouds. With the day turning gloomy, the boat moved into an area of dense fog with almost no visibility. Matt, who was at the wheel, suddenly pulled down the engine, reducing the noise around.

Ricardo walked up to the front end and stood next to him, trying to help out with an additional eye.

'That's alright, we're almost there.'

'How long is it to the airport?'

'Oh, I think it'll take us about 20 more minutes. It's a small island but we're on the other corner, you see.'

Saying that, Matt further reduced the power, and put the machine on idle. They entered in what seemed like a small lagoon covered by dense forests on all sides. The air was moist and the only sound was that of the boat pushing the water aside as it slowed down even further. Fog covered most of the area, though it was clear that the crew was closer to a jungle than a harbour.

'Where exactly are we?' Ricardo asked, a bit concerned.

'On the other side of civilisation,' Matt replied with a smile on his face.

Minutes later, the boat pulled up against a small weather-beaten, wooden quay. Matt pressed a small button on his console killing the engine as he jumped onto the wooden rest, holding a rope to the bow. He tied up the boat to a small horn fixed on the wooden wharf.

'Alright gentlemen, everyone off and walk this way please,' Matt shouted.

Korpovich walked up to Ricardo who was standing next to Matt. 'This just keeps getting better and better,' Korpovich said as Matt jumped onto the pier.

Ricardo followed as did the rest of the crew, helping each other with their bags as they moved. The area seemed to be pure jungle with no sign of habitation in sight. The direction Matt had pointed to was fully veiled by fog. After walking for a few minutes, they reached a small muddy road. A medium-sized black van was parked in the middle of the road.

'Everyone get into the back,' Matt shouted as he hopped into the driver's seat.

'I just told you, this keeps getting better and better!' Korpovich lamented as he got into the van.

Ricardo, on the other hand, stood firmly at the door, staring at the van as the rest of his companions got in, plonking their luggage in the centre.

'Need an invitation?' Korpovich shouted from inside the crowded van, mildly happy on reaching dry land.

Ricardo got into the van, closing the door behind him. The van roared to a start and got rolling, kicking dust as it moved. The dark interiors resembled a prison cell with no windows for natural light. A small lamp in the centre of the van roof emitted just about enough light to see the faces around.

The prison on wheels screeched its way to a solid road, burning rubber as it skid along a dangerous stretch. Half an hour later, it came to a sudden halt, shaking up the entire crew.

'Seems like we're there,' Korpovich looked at Ricardo sitting in a corner.

Ricardo did not reply.

The back door swung open and everyone was ready to hop off. Matt stood at the door looking in another direction. 'Give me a minute, I'll be right behind you,' he said to someone. Then he turned to the dark crowded interior and said, 'Alright, everybody listen. We're at the airport now. I'll go and get your passports stamped and then we'll be good to go.'

'You want us to come?' Korpovich asked, getting up from his seat. 'No, no, that won't be necessary. You guys stay put here and don't leave the van.' Matt banged the door shut and locked it from outside.

'Like I said, it keeps getting better and better!' Korpovich said plaintively.

Fifteen minutes went by.

'Where the hell is he?' Ricardo finally broke his silence.

'My guess is as good as yours,' Korpovich replied, shrugging his shoulders.

Ten minutes later, the door was unlocked again. Matt was back. 'Alright everybody, out. The flight takes off in 15 minutes.' He started pulling out the bags close to the door.

'What? Fifteen minutes, we haven't even been through the immigration yet. Is this the way airports are meant to function?' Korpovich exclaimed as he jumped out of the van and stretched his arms and legs.

'Don't worry, I've already had your passports stamped. All you have to do is board the plane,' Matt replied, pulling out a few more bags.

'I see!' Korpovich replied, puzzled at the young man's efficiency.

By now everyone was out. They followed Matt in a herd and soon entered a deserted alleyway which had a few conveyor belts on one side. Soon they came up to an entrance guarded by a lone armed guard. Matt walked up to him and exchanged a few words in Spanish. The guard looked at the bunch huddled together. Then he opened the door behind him to let them pass.

They entered a large hall which looked more like an airport than the earlier seedy alleyway. Counters of different airlines were lined up in the hall. At one of those counters, Matt handed over their passports individually, along with a ticket.

'Check your passports and tickets. All these flights are to your home towns. Everybody go straight to the counter ahead and follow the instructions. This is as far as I go,' said Matt with a big smile on his face.

The crew checked their passports, tickets, names and destinations. Everything was in order.

Half the crew picked up their bags and started to walk towards their flights. Korpovich and Ricardo picked up their bags and bid Matt goodbye.

'It was great sailing with you, sir. Learnt a lot from you,' Ricardo said politely.

'Oh come on boy! The pleasure was all mine,' Matt replied with a laugh. Ricardo and Korpovich hugged Matt warmly and walked off in the same direction as the rest of the crew.

Matt cast a final glance at the departing crew of the *Castle*. As he walked out of the departure hall, he took out his cell phone and called a number. 'Hey, it's Johan. Delivery completed. Get me out before anyone starts sniffing a rat.'

7

Investigations at Rio

Daylight was already spent when Ricardo arrived at the Rio International Airport. His flight had been short and lonely since he was the only member of the *Castle* flying to Brazil. Something about the whole episode troubled him. He decided to immediately report to the head office of International Marine in Rio and inquire about Captain Murthy. Ricardo cringed at the thought of leaving the old man behind on the *Castle*'s deck by a bright morning that had soon turned gloomy.

At the entrance of the building, he stopped short of the revolving glass door to think over what he was about to do. At the reception sat a beautiful lady in blue formals, surrounded by flickering computer screens. Ricardo took a deep breath and gave the door a forceful push before entering.

The massive lobby was lined with plush leather sofas. A few tables placed randomly were covered with application forms. It was moderate rush hour. Ricardo walked straight to the reception desk without looking left or right. He was not in a mood to run into acquaintances. He dumped his travel bag on the floor, drawing the beautiful lady's attention immediately. Ricardo's fine looks brought an instant smile on her face.

'How may I help you, sir?' she asked, staring at Ricardo's piercing blue eyes.

Ricardo replied in a well-rehearsed manner, 'Ricardo Pablo. I am here to see Steven please.'

'Just a moment, Mr Pablo,' the receptionist replied elegantly. Then turning to the computer she swiftly keyed in a name. She pressed the enter button and the computer started to scan the huge database for the name. While the computer was busy digging up history, she picked up the phone and dialled a short-key number. Within a second of receiving a response, she said, 'Steven, you have a guest.'

Then she turned to Ricardo and pointed across the hall, 'His office is down that alley.'

'Thank you,' Ricardo replied. He picked up his bag and headed towards Steven's office.

As she watched him disappear, her trance was interrupted by the beep of the computer indicating the search results were loaded. She turned to the computer screen, and turned pale. She looked back in the direction she had instructed Ricardo to take but could not see anyone. Immediately she picked up the phone and called Steven, 'Sir, we have a problem!'

~

Ricardo opened the cabin door slowly and entered. Dressed in black formals and a red striped necktie, Steven was peering over some data on the computer. The room was done up in wood and glass. The table had been pushed to one side to create more space. The floor was covered with light brown fur carpet.

From the corner of his eye, Steven saw Ricardo walk in. 'Hi young man, have a seat.' Steven was so engrossed in his work that he didn't think about the man who had just walked in. Seconds later, he jumped up from his chair in shock, 'Ricardo Pablo, is that you! What are you doing here?'

'I just got in. The ship was handed over,' Ricardo started to explain but Steven cut him short.

'What?' he shouted. He picked up the phone and was about to dial a number when his cabin door swung open.

An elderly man in formals stood at the door. The general manager of the Rio branch of International Marine, SJS Cardoze held a sheet of paper in his hand.

'Sir, I was about to call you,' Steven said in a panic.

Cardoze looked at Ricardo, then at the sheet of paper in his hand as he walked in.

'What's going on here?' he asked Steven sternly.

'I wanted to ask you the same question,' Steven replied.

Both of them looked enquiringly at each other, before turning to Ricardo.

'What?' Ricardo wondered what was going on.

'When did you come here?' Cardoze asked.

'I just got out of the airport. We handed over the ship at Curaçao and everyone went back home. I thought I'll drop by here before I head home too. What's wrong with that?'

His words confirmed Steven and Cardoze's worst fears. The old man slowly walked up to the door and shut it. He seemed lost in thought as he walked back towards Steven who looked worried. 'Call the Indian office and ask them about this. Also notify the owners immediately. I'll call the P&I Club,' Cardoze said calmly.

'Excuse me, sir. What's going on?' Ricardo asked.

Cardoze turned to Ricardo and said, 'We didn't hand over any ship in Curaçao!'

~

Two hours had passed since Ricardo had told them about what had happened. Their panic mounted with each passing second. The *Castle* was nowhere to be found.

Cardoze had been on his toes since then and Steven's office had become the coordination centre for this case. Cardoze sat in Steven's chair talking on his cell phone. Ricardo sat in a corner. All along, he had suspected something was amiss.

A female employee barged into the room. Everyone looked at her hopefully.

'What is it?' Cardoze asked her.

'It's the satellite phone, sir. I have been trying for almost two hours, and there still isn't any response,' she said politely.

'Well, then call the bloody INMARSAT office and find out what the hell is wrong with their phone,' he yelled back.

'I've already called them, sir. They say they can't do anything about this. It's a local error,' she replied meekly.

'Then keep trying!' Cardoze snapped back angrily.

'Yes, sir. Sorry, sir,' she left the room hastily, closing the door behind her.

Cardoze took a deep breath then got back on the phone, 'I'm really sorry. Where was I?'

After a few minutes of intense discussion with his interlocutor, Cardoze got up, slipping the phone into his pocket. He looked dissatisfied with the discussion. Running his fingers through his hair, he looked at Steven, 'Inform the police and the press. We need both to locate the *Castle*.'

Cardoze had thought the matter could be sorted out internally, but deep down he knew that that was no longer possible. If the police were brought in, all the news channels would be clamouring for him like hounds, tearing away at his spotless life. No company wanted negative publicity in the media, but things had gotten out of hand now.

'Cops! Are you sure, sir?' Steven inquired.

'Of course, I'm sure,' Cardoze shot back. 'We can't lie low for long. The ship was supposed to be in Ecuador in two days. The receivers will be jumping off the roof if we don't issue a statement.'

Steven got the point. He was thinking of a story. They had to give the media a clear picture.

'We'll tell them it's a case of hijacking. The owners have already initiated an investigation. It is an international issue now. Too many people are involved, and I'm not even talking of the culprits yet!' Cardoze sounded more composed this time.

Steven didn't say anything. Ricardo, however, tried to remember everything that had happened on board. 'I don't think it's a case of hijacking, you see...' Ricardo had barely begun when Cardoze interrupted him. 'No need to think on your own. You say what we tell you to say and keep away from any sort of media. I hope I've made myself clear.'

Ricardo did not have any option. 'Yes sir,' he said obediently.

'Good, now the cops are on their way. You might be required to give some statements. Do as they say,' Cardoze hissed.

'Alright,' replied Ricardo.

Minutes later, a black Mercedes sedan with tinted glass and a siren on the roof, pulled up at the main gate of the International Marine head office.

Two men stepped out of the car and walked up to the glass door. One of them wore a black formal suit, his gun strapped to his chest, intentionally visible, while the other official, far more senior, was dressed in off-white semi-formals. He walked up briskly to the reception, the sound of his shoes echoing in the hall. 'Good morning, Miss. I'm here to see Mr Cardoze,' he said, taking off his black aviators.

'Yes sir, may I have your name please?' the lady at the reception asked softly.

'Most certainly. It's Carlos, Chief Inspector José Carlos.'

8

A Ship Changes Hands

What had seemed to be an unusually quick handover of a ship now seemed to be a conspiracy. International Marine portrayed it as a case of hijacking, but Ricardo knew better. He sat in a moderate-sized room, expensively done up in hues of brown. The mahogany furniture was set on parquet flooring. In the centre, a large desk occupied most of the space, with well-cushioned chairs around it. A fluffy sofa occupied a corner. Two overhead lamps shone brightly above the table. This was Chief Inspector José Carlos's office at the police headquarters. The hijacking story had been running on all the news channels since morning.

Ricardo's statement had to be recorded. He waited for his hosts. Carlos entered, accompanied by another middle-aged man. Each one carried a couple of files. Carlos walked across to the large table while the other man settled down on the fluffy sofa, placing the files on the table in front of him. Carlos eased himself into the huge cushioned chair and looked at Ricardo as he put three cell phones on his table.

'I didn't realise we would meet here like this, with you on that side of the desk,' Carlos needed to get the witness talking.

'Yeah, and I certainly didn't think you'd be on that side either,' Ricardo replied, trying to make light of the conversation.

'I bet you didn't,' Carlos looked at Ricardo suspiciously. Then he opened one of the many files on his table and looking at the papers, spoke formally, 'As you know, the ship you were on is now missing. We have told the press that it might have been hijacked, but that is only to gain more time for the investigation. As this is an international matter now, a multinational team has been set up to solve the case.'

He closed the file and pushed his weight back on the chair, rolling it back a few inches. Looking at the third person in the room, he continued, 'A team of three people has been set up for this case. Me, you already know. The second person is this gentleman here, Mr. Enrique Roberto from Panama Federal Bureau as the ship was of Panamanian nationality and a third person who is…'

Carlos was still speaking when a young man knocked. Without waiting for an answer, he entered the office, 'Hello sir, sorry I'm late.'

'...Mr. Anshul Jaitley from India, as your missing Captain is from that part of the world,' Carlos spoke, pointing at the young man.

'AJ sir. You can call me AJ,' he responded with a modest smile.

A well-built Indian in his late twenties, fair with thick black hair, light brown eyes and sharp features, AJ was dressed casually. Known to be a thorough professional, AJ had never been to Brazil before. Roberto and Carlos had worked together on a few cases in the past and knew each other well.

The young man sat next to Roberto who was busy studying his files.

Ricardo looked around. 'Nice team you got here. What can I do now? I've already given my statement,' he added.

'I know that Ricardo, but you are all we have right now,' Carlos seemed annoyed with Ricardo.

'So what do you have in mind?' Ricardo asked.

'Need to know everything we possibly can to solve this puzzle.' As he finished, Carlos got up from his seat and walked to the middle of the room. 'Alright people, listen. We have already met each other. This young man here is Ricardo.'

AJ and Ricardo shook hands and turned back to Carlos.

'We have already received statements from around the globe and the picture isn't that good. Roberto will do the minutes now. Roberto…'

Carlos stepped aside and Roberto took centre stage. He walked up and down the office as he spoke, 'So here's the story. A ship sails happily from Brazil to Ecuador. On the way, they find a stowaway and lock her up. Yes, a girl, a rather beautiful one as Ricardo here has stated. Then all of a sudden, Captain Rajan Murthy tells everyone that the ship is being handed over because a stowaway has been discovered aboard. They divert to Curaçao, eastern side, which, by the way, is mostly deserted. There they meet agents, cops and everyone else who don't exist! Then everyone is sent home from the airport with immigration clearance which a man named Matt gets for them. This man here flies back to Rio and then we all start fretting about plugging all the loopholes and figuring out the missing connective tissues in this neatly woven narrative.' Roberto finished his minutes and chucked his files to one side.

Leaning against the glass window, as Roberto spoke, Carlos reflected deeply. 'AJ, what after that?'

Sitting in the corner chair, Ricardo seemed lost in thought. He was more amused than curious as this was the first time he was witnessing a legal investigation unfold.

AJ got up from the sofa and cleared his throat. 'After all that action, the company has come out with the idea of a hijacking, which I personally feel is ridiculous. Anyway, reports from all the crew members read pretty much the same. As far as the current status is concerned, government authorities in Curaçao have given a statement saying that they have no information of any such activity. In short, they are more lost than we are. Either they are pretending to be dumb or they really are. How could so much have happened right under their noses without them getting the whiff of it?

'Getting back to the point, the stowaway is missing with the ship. From the sketch, she has been identified as Daze Cartia from Panama. Her history? Not too encouraging I'd like to add. I'm sure Roberto would have more to say on that.'

Roberto turned to the group, 'She was born and brought up in Panama in an orphanage. Ran away when she was 15 and has been registered in almost 18 cases of involvement with local gangs.'

Ricardo seemed shocked, 'She looked rather harmless to me!' His heart reached out to her. How similar his and Daze's life had been, at least in part.

'I am just going by the records and the records are correct Ricardo, but any particular reason for your soft approach?' asked Carlos.

'Well, not really, all I mean to say is that she didn't really create much trouble. That's all.'

Carlos gave a smile. He knew more than he was letting on.

AJ continued, 'Besides the girl, we have two agents who took these guys off the ship. Now, as the authorities in Curaçao have said, they have no idea about what happened. Now who would believe that? Even our database can't identify any of these men. For all we know, they could have been ghosts.'

In the midst of AJ's briefing, one of Carlos's phones rang. He heard the caller for almost a minute before hanging up. Then he turned to the crowd and announced, 'There is some urgent work I need to attend to. Everyone do your homework and we'll meet at Mirage Café at seven.'

Everyone nodded.

'And Ricardo, try to remember as much as you can till then.' Carlos patted him on the back before leaving the room.

Ricardo sighed, looking at the two men picking up their files, 'All I can remember? Now what more could I have missed out on?'

~

With each passing hour, the mystery of the *Castle* deepened. It was already 48 hours that the vessel had gone missing and nobody knew where to look for it.

The sun bid adieu to yet another day. It was peak traffic time with office-goers heading back home. This was the hour when the local café's did brisk business. All eat-outs were packed to capacity. And the topic *du jour* was the mystery of the missing *Castle*.

Mirage Café was one of the many economical eat-outs in downtown Rio and extremely popular for its prompt service. As the clock struck seven, the near-full café seemed to get even more crowded.

Ricardo sat with Roberto and AJ next to a small table near the entrance. A fourth chair had been reserved for Carlos who was running late.

The café was done up in ethnic chic with generous splashes of maroons and light browns. Huge posters of different coffee beans, coffee-brewing regions and coffee mugs hung on all walls. The heady aroma of Arabica added to the appeal of the interiors. Big cushioned chairs were casually strewn about. Television sets were mounted on all sides to ensure a view from every seat. All the sets were tuned to the same channel running the evening news. A young female reporter was reading the news briskly in English. Most of her words went unheard till she reached the main story of the day. 'According to our updates on Motor Vessel *Castle*, the owners have made it clear that the vessel has been hijacked and the police are backing that version too. There have been no further updates by the concerned authorities till now. The Commissioner of Police stated that an international investigation unit has been set up as requested by the Panamanian government, the flag state of the missing ship. The authorities are expecting quick results in this case. However, there have been no comments on the case by the investigating unit till now.'

Roberto and AJ shuddered at the thought of being accosted by a group of reporters at this hour.

The reporter continued, 'While all clues point to a possible theft, the owners have summarily rejected all such speculations and have come out in complete support of the missing Indian captain.'

As she spoke her last line, the channel aired the footage of the media conference which had taken place at the International Marine's head office earlier in the day. 'Reportedly, the ship was last seen off the Island of Curaçao in the Caribbean region. Government authorities in Curaçao have issued a short statement saying that they have no information about the vessel and that it was not supposed to enter their territorial waters without prior permission. They are looking into the matter. Although there has been no confirmation, some believe that the authorities in the small Caribbean country might be involved in the hijacking of the Panamanian bulker. Strangely, the crew on board the vessel was officially signed off before she went missing—one of the many curious aspects of this mystery.

he black market, there is sensitive nuclear for grabs. Now this is really big. The price it ted to fetch is around USD 2 billion. I have ed news that the Chinese and Japanese are g over it,' AJ spoke in a hushed tone.

t the net value of the ship with the cargo is ted at around USD 2.3 billion,' Roberto joined in iratorially.

es, I know. But there is a twist. While the source of ata is not new to the market, the carrier definitely irst-timer, and they refer to him as Captain.'

Ricardo, who was listening carefully, stopped ing his coffee and looked at AJ. Who was Captain? ... the table breaking the minute-

'In another developn

The crowd in the café

topic. Carlos entered look

up to the vacant chair and

Everyone else at the table wa

to say something.

'Did I miss anything?' C

everyone sitting on the table.

'Besides the direct attack on th

nothing much,' AJ replied as he si

A waitress holding a small pa

at the table to take the order. Carlo

said, 'I'll have an Irish coffee with

knew the menu by heart.

'In t

data up

is expec

confirm

warrin

'Bu

estima

consp

'Y

the d

is a f

sipp

side of comfort. As the sun rose in the sky, its golden glow was slowly obscured by the clouds. The powerful roar of the V8 engine of a black Audi, with tinted glasses, shattered the silence as the car zipped onto the half-constructed wharf at the seaward end. The luxury wheels turned towards the edge of the breakwater to enter a locale which was a perfect foil to the sleeping world outside.

Workers gathered on the wharf as the car came to a halt. Dressed in a black semi-formal suit, Tro stepped out of the car. The sight in front of his eyes held him in thrall. The *Castle* was tied to the berth. She was much bigger than he had imagined. He had done it. His plan had worked. But this was only the beginning. The master stroke was still to be executed.

'Tro! Welcome to Montserrat,' said Caster, the man who had introduced himself as the agent in Curaçao. He had taken the vessel thereon and sailed her to Little Bay. Dressed in casuals topped with a coffee-coloured knee-length overcoat, he greeted Tro with a half hug. Caster had been working for Tro for longer than he could remember and was one of his trusted allies in some of the top secret operations. The man standing beside him in the light brown leather overcoat was Captain Murthy.

Tro walked up to Murthy and shook his hands. Murthy felt a little self-conscious as he had never been in a gathering of criminals and masterminds before. With a reluctant smile, he returned the gesture.

'Finally we meet, Captain,' Tro smiled.

'Yes, it's a pleasure. You look much younger than I had expected,' Murthy replied with a laugh.

'I'll take that as a compliment,' said Tro as he turned to Caster. 'What is the status?' They started to walk in a group.

'All good, sir. As you had wished, the painters will start painting it in a few minutes,' Caster replied.

'And the data?' Tro asked sternly.

'That's been taken care of. Just as you had instructed,' Caster replied in a hushed whisper.

9

Piecing Together a Puzzle

It was just another day as the airbus from Rio landed at Curaçao International Airport, bringing with it the high-profile team investigating the disappearance of the *Castle*. As the flight came to a halt in front of the main exit gate, everyone reached for their bags in the overhead cabins. The flight attendant announced the local time and bid farewell to the passengers with a good word about the temperature outside. The clock had already struck nine by the time the gates opened.

Carlos and his team were travelling business class. A young air hostess pulled out their bags for them. All three investigators were dressed in black suits and off-white shirts. Ricardo, however, was dressed casually in a pair of jeans and a linen shirt. As they got up to leave, AJ turned to Ricardo, 'So what do they call the people here, Curacies or Curacaoians?'

'Frankly, I have no clue!' Ricardo laughed.

As they walked out of Curaçao International Airport, they saw an old man holding up a board: 'Inspector José Carlos, welcome to Curaçao.'

The old man had been serving as a guide for the local police for a few years and didn't mind wearing his hair and beard grey. He was accompanied by a relatively young, stern-looking man dressed in a green military uniform.

As soon as Carlos spotted his name, he walked up to the merrier of the two men, followed by the rest of the team. He was about to say something to greet the old man when the man in uniform stepped forward and said, 'Good morning, sir, welcome to Curaçao.'

'Good morning. I'm Inspector Carlos and these are my associates here,' he pointed to the group behind him.

'We are aware of that, sir. I am here on behalf of the Curaçao National Guard. I have been sent to remind you that you have been granted a 24-hour window for this visit, starting now. I believe you already have your return tickets booked for tomorrow morning's 9 a.m. flight out of here.' Then pointing to Francisco, he added, 'This man here will be your guide and contact for your stay here. In short, he goes where you go. Do you have any questions, sir?'

'I think I'm good for now. Thanks for the hospitality,' Carlos replied politely, but curtly.

Without saying another word, the young man turned around and walked off to a military vehicle parked across the road and drove off.

The old man laughed and turned to Carlos, 'Don't worry about that. I'm Francisco, your driver, guide and I think your only friend in this town.'

'I figured that out,' AJ quipped.

Francisco smiled as he turned to Carlos again, 'So, time is short. What's the plan?'

'Can you take us to the crime scene?' Carlos enquired.

'There isn't a place on this island where Francisco can't take you,' he winked as he held the car door open for his guests.

Everyone got into the backseat while Carlos sat in front, next to Francisco.

The place seemed sparsely populated. The only people visible on the streets clearly looked like tourists in colourful short clothes.

'How far is the place?' Carlos asked casually.

'About 20 minutes from here,' Ricardo shouted abruptly from the backseat.

'You've been here before?' Francisco asked a little surprised.

Carlos immediately cut in, 'Yes, he has. So Francisco, is there any investigation going on?' He tried to change the topic.

'I wish there was one,' Francisco replied as he stepped on the accelerator.

After driving for almost 15 minutes, the car veered off onto a half-constructed road which slowly transformed into a gravel stretch smoothened by passing vehicles. Occasional patches of lush grass and stray shrubs bordered it.

Carlos interrogated Francisco throughout the ride but the driver didn't seem to mind. 'Are we there yet?'

'Nope, just five more minutes,' Francisco replied.

In the rear view mirror, Francisco saw the other wide-eyed travellers. But it was Ricardo who drew his attention.

Ricardo's mind wandered back to the black prison van. The crew of the *Castle* couldn't see these beautiful surroundings. He remembered turning to another person sitting quietly in one corner of that cramped van. Jason had a grim look on his face. He was scared. Where was Matt taking them? Then he saw Ricardo studying his reactions carefully, and turned his face away.

Ricardo wiped the sweat off his forehead as he returned from the past, to catch Francisco staring at him through the rear-view mirror.

'You guys have any leads yet?' Francisco asked.

'A few but nothing substantial.' As Chief Inspector and an investigating officer, Carlos knew how to keep his answers short.

'Do you think the Captain did it?' Francisco asked casually.

Judging by the surprise on everyone's face, Francisco offered a quick clarification, 'I watch the news, like all of you.'

The car entered a patch where dense tree canopies cut off the skies, but for the odd beams of light that dodged the lush green overhead carpet to hit the ground. The fragrance of the moist jungle drifted into the car as it snaked its way around trees and bushes into the heart of darkness.

Francisco switched on the headlights. After a few more sharp turns and curves, the car pulled up near a small lagoon which had been cordoned off by yellow warning tape suspended from the surrounding trees. As soon as the car came to a halt, everyone hopped out quietly. The forest bed was full of rainwater puddles, perhaps from frequent showers.

The investigators fanned out in different directions. Ricardo set off towards the small wooden wharf in the distance. He had been here just the other day. As he reached the end of the wharf, he tried to recollect the whole episode. Carlos kept a close watch on him. Francisco leaned against the bonnet of the car.

'This place is a mess,' Carlos popped up behind him.

'We had thundershowers yesterday. We get those frequently on this end of the island,' Francisco replied.

thought of the times when he had sat on the beaches of Recife to watch the sun meet the horizon. Suddenly tears welled up in his eyes.

Carlos opened the door without warning and announced, 'It's time.' Then he left without waiting for an answer from the man in the balcony.

Ricardo stood fixed in his place with his hands in his pocket. He shut his eyes and took a deep breath to bring himself back to reality. As he opened his eyes, he turned around slowly, looked at the door and whispered to himself almost prophetically, 'Yes, it's time.'

~

The car pulled up into an open air parking lot with dense forests on one side, and a huge board on the other side, with 'Campo Allegre' written in multi-coloured glow lights.

'Alright gentlemen, this is as far as I go.' There was fear in Francisco's voice.

'Not even for a beer?' Carlos held out a bait.

Francisco didn't bite it. 'Try and stay out of trouble,' he cautioned everyone as they hopped off.

They split up into two groups. They had to, to avoid raising suspicion. Carlos walked ahead with AJ while Ricardo and Roberto fell behind. They reached the entrance to find it barred by a steel door secured by an electronic lock. Two tall and well-built Africans in black denims and skin tight black T-shirts with 'Security' printed across the chest, looked ready to kill.

Without uttering a word, one of them directed Carlos to a small window, manned by a young girl, to the left of the gate. Carlos slipped in a 20-dollar bill and the girl pressed a few keys on a small digital pad in front of her. As she pressed the enter key, the electronic lock was released, and the entrance door swung open. Carlos lead the way. The same guard stepped forward and said gruffly, 'Spread out your hands, please.'

Both guests complied. The guards finished the routine frisking and stepping back, let them into the club with a tepid, 'Welcome to Campo Allegre.'

A few yards down a narrow corridor, they entered a totally different world. The huge hall, packed with nattily dressed ladies and men, was criss-crossed by flashing red and green laser beams. In the centre was a huge circular bar. At one end were a few pool tables and some slot machines. Huge plasma screens on the walls ran the same fashion channel. Popular hip-hop fare played at an unimaginable decibel. The crowd inside seemed as Francisco had said—rich and powerful. As Carlos and AJ moved towards the bar, they were greeted with seductive smiles.

'I've never felt more wanted in my entire life,' AJ whispered into Carlos's ear.

The dimly lit bar was designed in black, with glasses of all shapes and sizes suspended overhead. The stylish column at the centre was lined with expensive liquor and wines.

A young boy with spiked blonde hair and a black stud in his left ear came up from behind the counter, 'Your order, please?'

'Two JD's on the rocks,' said AJ without asking Carlos.

Within seconds, the bartender served up the order in thick crystal glasses lined with sugar and topped with ice.

As Carlos picked up his glass, Roberto and Ricardo passed by without even looking at him. Both headed for the dance floor, moving swiftly through the crowd, looking for familiar faces. Roberto was relying on Ricardo for leads. The laser lights and the loud hip hop music kept distracting Roberto.

Ricardo searched desperately for a familiar face. All the faces he had come across in the last three days flashed past before his eyes as he tried to look for a needle in a desert. An hour went by without much success. As Ricardo was about to give up, he thought he saw a man who looked very familiar. He was dressed in a black shirt and brown trousers, holding a beer in one hand. As the man moved on the dance floor, a pretty young Venezuelan matched his steps.

'Roberto, that's Matt. The fellow who took us from the ship to the airport,' hissed Ricardo, his eyes fixed on his find.

Immediately Roberto started walking towards the mark. Ricardo followed him cautiously, trying to spot Carlos in the crowd, but before he could find him, Matt and his friend had moved away from the hall and were walking in an alley bordered by small huts. As the music faded in the background, Roberto closed distance between himself, Matt and his friend. Ricardo was still hoping to find Carlos and AJ somewhere, when Roberto, now within yards of Matt and his friend, shouted, 'Hi there, mate!'

Matt slowly turned around, but before he knew, Roberto punched him hard on the jaw. Matt was flung back before landing on the ground. The young girl screamed as she saw blood oozing from her companion's nose. Roberto didn't pay any heed and pulled the injured man back on his feet.

'Hello Matt, remember my friend here. He's been missing you a lot,' Roberto sneered, trying to make Matt remember.

'What the f**k are you talking about, man! My name's Johan,' said the man gingerly, touching his bloodied face.

'Really? Did I punch you that hard?' he continued, as he held Matt by his collar, almost lifting him off the ground.

red Chinese sticker on the front bumper rolled in. Its heavily tinted glasses made it impossible to see anything inside. The car stopped in front of the warehouse. Tro, accompanied by Caster and another man, walked swiftly up to the car.

General Lee stepped out from the backseat, accompanied by a security guard, and greeted Tro, 'Hello, dear friend! It is indeed a pleasure meeting again.' Then he fixed his gaze on the *Trader*, breathed in deeply and smile.

'I hope the journey wasn't too much of a bother,' Tro enquired politely.

'Not at all, but why the sudden change of plans? Not that I mind, it's completely your prerogative,' General Lee observed.

'Well, I felt it was a better option to do the deal here,' Tro answered, stressing on 'here.'

'About the money, I have...' General Lee started, but was interrupted by Tro. 'You mind if I ask you a personal question.'

'Please go ahead,' General Lee grew uncomfortable.

'Why is that you Chinese think that I'm a bloody idiot?' Tro was visibly angry.

'I don't understand. Is there a problem? Do you find the deal to be inadequate?' General Lee was confused.

'Inadequate?' Tro smirked. 'The problem is that you tried to sell me out to the bloody cops.'

General Lee remained silent. He was taking stock of the situation.

Caster pointed a gun to the General's head. Tro followed suit as did all the other guards patrolling the area. The General's security guard whipped out a mini revolver and trained it on Tro's head. The Chinese driver leapt out of the car wielding a shotgun as he shielded himself behind the open door.

General Lee raised a hand signalling his men to back off. 'We must not take hasty decisions. I'm sure there has been a misunderstanding.'

'There was a misunderstanding. It's crystal clear now,' Tro shot back.

'What can I do to convince you that there is no such conspiracy?' asked General Lee trying to ease the tension.

After a pause, Tro said, 'Nothing.'

The guards on the roof of the warehouse pressed the trigger. Two bullets tore through space and hit the two Chinese guards on their temples. Fresh blood splattered across the windshield. Instantly, they fell to the ground.

General Lee stared at the dead men. Then he turned to Tro. 'It is shocking to see how easily you have been misled by the Japanese, Tro. And I thought you were a man of good judgement.'

'Save the speech General, you've had your chance,' Tro replied.

'You think you can trust them. They will trick you into your own death and you won't even have a clue,' General Lee opined.

Tro listened carefully before saying, 'I know.'

10

An Unexpected Arrest

At the end of 24 hours, the investigators took the morning flight back to Rio. They had found a positive lead, or so they thought. In the next media conference, Carlos planned to give out the Captain's name as one of the prime suspects. But that wasn't going to be easy.

'What about the company's stand? They are still trying to back Murthy,' Roberto said to Carlos as they walked out of the airport.

'It's about time they faced the truth. Besides, we all know it's for the insurance. I guess they'll have to take this beating,' Carlos replied casually.

'They'll get something from the insurance, won't they?' AJ queried.

Carlos just smiled without saying anything. As they walked towards a small group of police cars parked in a corner, Carlos looked over his shoulder at Ricardo, who seemed lost in another world.

'You haven't spoken a word on the flight back. What are you thinking of?' Carlos broke in, bringing Ricardo back to reality.

'Oh, nothing. Just felt strange going back to the same place, that's all.'

Carlos waited for Ricardo to say something more. Then he ordered one of the policemen who had come to fetch them, 'Arrest him.'

'What!' Ricardo shouted, completely taken aback.

Before he could react, he was pinned down to the bonnet of a black Land Rover and handcuffed.

'What's going on, Carlos? Is this some kind of a game?' he shouted desperately.

'No Ricardo, the game's over. I gave you time. This is what you chose,' said Carlos, just as the policemen shoved Ricardo into the backseat of the SUV and banged the door shut.

~

Ricardo had been sitting for more than three hours waiting for somebody to walk in with the answers. The room with just one steel door was poorly ventilated. There was a small table in the middle and another wooden chair. Ricardo hadn't changed his clothes since the last visit to Curaçao and his hair was as messed up as his mind. He had no clue why all of a sudden Carlos had turned upon him.

Outside the headquarters, Carlos and his team were surrounded by press reporters and cameramen. He stood behind a podium, ready to brief the press about the *Castle* investigations. The sky was overcast and a cold breeze had kicked in. It would drizzle any moment.

'That's correct, we have just returned from an official visit to Curaçao and as I have made it clear before, we are certain the Government of Curaçao is not involved,' Carlos spoke confidently.

'As far as the case is concerned, we have made some progress in the matter, but we would still request the media to be patient about the outcome as the case is very sensitive and involves various administrations. So far, our investigations seem to clearly indicate that this is a case of theft, and not hijacking.

'We have identified the suspects and we believe that the Master onboard the ship at the time of the theft, Captain Rajan Krishnamurthy, is one of the prime suspects. All administrations have been informed and an internationally coordinated search has been mounted in this respect.'

The reporters jotted down every word. Carlos's revelation came as a surprise.

'At this point, we would appreciate any information whatsoever on him from any source. That would be all for now,' Carlos hurried away from the podium into the headquarters without waiting to take any questions.

AJ and Roberto followed him into the building. Carlos walked swiftly into the waiting elevator with AJ and Roberto. He pressed the button for the fourth floor.

Roberto broke the silence, 'I still don't understand. Why Ricardo?'

'We're about to find out,' Carlos replied as the elevator sped up to the fourth floor and the doors slid open. 'I'll see you in my cabin.'

Carlos walked up to the steel door with a small sliding window. He waited outside, preparing himself for a few seconds before walking into the cell where Ricardo sat on a wooden chair in front of a centre table. Carlos sat on the empty chair.

'Is there anything you'd like to say before I start?' Carlos asked.

'I'm not saying anything without my lawyer,' Ricardo spat back.

Carlos continued unperturbed, 'Good, then it's my turn. I came across a very nice young man... A Filipino. Jason. Heard of him?'

Ricardo didn't say anything.

'Well, I'll remind you if you've forgotten.' Carlos continued, 'He was on the *Castle*.'

'I know who he is. What's the point you are making?' Ricardo interrupted.

'My point is that he happened to tell the police that he saw a murder on board,' Carlos shouted back.

Ricardo was taken back by this piece of information.

Carlos moved, leaning forward as he spoke softly, 'A murder that you were a part of.'

'That's not true,' Ricardo replied in a whisper. 'I didn't do anything.'

'If you were innocent, why didn't you tell me about the murder. What do I make of this?' Carlos looked at Ricardo.

'I didn't do anything,' Ricardo replied. 'I don't know what Jason saw. I was just standing there. It was Murthy…he shot the guy. Believe me, it was him.'

'How can I believe you now?' Carlos looked dejected. 'You had your chance to tell the whole truth but you chose not to. I have been running around looking for a clue when the bloody witness was right under my nose.'

'I wanted to tell you. I thought I would,' Ricardo started, but was cut short by Carlos.

'Then why didn't you?' yelled Carlos.

'It's because of Murthy.' For the first time, Ricardo was nervous. 'He threatened to have me killed if I said anything. And when I reached here, I thought I'd tell you everything but I was too scared. I didn't know what to do, so I kept quiet. Like an idiot, I kept quiet. Now he'll think that I sold him out and he's going to come after me,' Ricardo sounded disturbed.

'There's much more to you than you show Ricardo,' Carlos sighed as he got up to leave. Just as Carlos reached the door and turned the knob, Ricardo said, 'There's much more to you as well, Carlos, than meets the eye.' Carlos stopped and turned around, holding the door half open. The sudden change in Ricardo made him uncomfortable.

'What do you mean?' Carlos asked sharply.

'Back in Curaçao, when we had pinned down Johan, you arrived five minutes later with AJ, and called him Johan. Nobody told you his real name was Johan…and not Matt,' Ricardo challenged Carlos.

Carlos looked at Ricardo for a minute without saying anything, then he slowly shut the door and walked back towards Ricardo.

~

The town woke up to every channel airing updates on the theft of the *Castle*. Roberto and Carlos were among the millions tuned in as they sat in Carlos's office at the headquarters.

On the television screen, a young girl sitting stiffly reported in fluent English, 'Minutes after the investigation team in Rio declared the involvement of the Master, Captain Rajan Krishnamurthy, in the theft of the vessel, M.V. *Castle*, the Indian authorities joined in, strongly criticising the actions of the Indian

Master. The Indian government has offered full support and an Indian officer is already a part of the three-member investigation team in charge of the case. The government spokesperson in a media meet has said that such offences will not be taken lightly and strong action will be taken against those involved. Interestingly, this is the first time an Indian seafarer has been involved in such a case. The United Nations offshoot, IMO, has expressed deep anguish over the incident, and has offered to help bring the culprits to book.'

That was followed by a video footage of what looked like a press conference. The logo on the wall behind the speaker said International Maritime Organisation. The man in his late fifties spoke in a polished British accent, 'The involvement of the Master has shamed the entire industry and forced us to bring in new measures so that such incidents do not occur again. We are in touch with the concerned authorities and the matter is being monitored very closely as it has international ramifications.'

Carlos switched off the television and chucked the remote on the sofa besides Roberto. Leaning back on his chair, he asked Roberto, 'If you stole a ship, where would you go?'

'Where would I go? Not to the cops for sure. Maybe somewhere...where I can hide it for some time.' Roberto wondered if that was the right answer.

'He's hiding for sure. By now the ship would have been sold off to whoever wanted it and our man has more money than he could have ever earned,' Carlos spoke with certitude.

'Of course there would have been a buyer before the whole plan was executed. I mean you don't steal a ship and take it to the market,' Roberto added.

'Yes, that's true and what is important is to find the big fish. Murthy is just a pawn in this game. There are much bigger players out there.' Carlos would get to those guys.

'What's cooking for Ricardo?' Roberto asked uneasily.

'Nothing, I've moved him to the witness protection cell for the moment. He claims Murthy threatened to have him bumped off,' Carlos said matter-of-factly.

'You mean he's under house arrest?'

'You can say that. Where the hell is AJ?' Carlos tried to change the topic.

'Out hunting. One of his informants came through with some big news. Looks like we might have a lead,' Roberto said seriously.

Roberto had barely finished when AJ walked in and sat down in front of Carlos.

'Good morning, AJ,' Carlos seemed surprised.

'Good morning,' AJ replied as he picked up the glass of water on the table and gulped it down in one go. 'Alright, big news. You remember I had told you about the mega deal priced at about USD 2 billion. Well our man, Captain Rajan Murthy, is the front man for some big gun.'

'But the ship is not worth that much!' Roberto was puzzled.

'I know. It's not the ship they are selling.' AJ clarified. 'Someone's selling blueprints of their country's nuclear programme. The ship is just a cover-up for the whole thing.'

'Are you sure about this?' Carlos asked.

'Definite news, the data is probably going to the Chinese but the Japanese are strong contenders as well,' AJ confirmed.

'You mean the Yakuza?' Roberto asked.

AJ nodded without saying anything.

'What about the actual seller? Do we have any clue?' Carlos asked.

'Nothing, it's a loop. If you start looking for the source, you end up where you started. Right now all we can figure out is that Murthy is the front man. And I checked it up with the intelligence data. It all fits perfectly,' AJ replied.

Carlos was already assessing the update. Then he picked up the phone and said authoritatively, 'Get me the Defence Secretary. Tell him it's urgent.'

Just then, a young officer barged in, 'Sir, urgent update. We've just heard from the US coastguard. The *Castle*'s EPIRB has been activated in the Pacific, about 50 miles off Panama. They are sending in their rescue teams now.'

'What's EPIRB?' AJ asked innocently.

'Emergency position indicating radio beacon,' Carlos enlightened him. 'It's supposed to get activated if the ship sinks,' Roberto was concerned.

'The ship sinks...? You mean...' AJ trailed off.

Minutes after the sudden turn of events, Carlos entered a small room loaded with radio equipment and computers. Three female operators sitting across the room jumped to their feet as they saw the chief walk in. He asked for the moderately sized high-range radio mounted on the wall. The handset was already connected to the US coastguard busy coordinating the rescue operation off Panama.

'Good afternoon Captain, thank you for holding the rescue. This is Chief Inspector Carlos speaking,' Carlos spoke slowly and clearly.

'That's alright, Inspector. Can you give me any insight on this?' the man asked professionally.

'Captain, this is not a rescue operation. The ship has been missing for almost a week now and this could well be a trap. I suggest you go in carefully and I'd prefer to stay online if you don't have any objection,' Carlos replied speaking faster this time.

'Certainly not. Let's go fishing,' the man replied casually as he put the radio on standby.

On Carlos's advice, two choppers loaded with armed marines tore through the sky to the beacon position. The marines were dressed in military gear with digital gear on their back and heat-sensing eyepieces. They held combat weapons firmly in hand as they crouched in the back of the helicopter.

As the choppers approached the RV position, they spotted their target—a small wooden fishing boat, dead still in the middle of nowhere. They moved in a circular formation, hovering over the small boat covered with a hay roof in the centre and a canvas in the aft. The turbulence from the choppers disturbed the sea beneath as air rushed outward rocking the boat. No movement could be seen on the small craft as the choppers moved around for a clearer view from all possible angles. Finally the pilot in one of the choppers pressed his radio and spoke, 'Base, this is Rescue hound Alpha, we are at the LZ and we have the target in sight. Request permission to engage, over.'

The Base answered without delay as Carlos, sitting tense in front of the radio set in Rio, listened in.

'Rescue hound Alpha, this is Base. You have permission to engage. Proceed to the target carefully.

I repeat, proceed carefully, over,' the mission coordinator replied.

'Roger that Base, we're going in now, over and out,' the pilot added as he turned to the marines sitting at the back and shouted enthusiastically, 'Alright men, rock 'n' roll.'

Before the pilot could finish speaking, marines from both the choppers threw out high strength crocodile ropes. One of the marines hanging off the rope shut his eyes, remembering God.

On the pilot's signal, they jumped outboard and slid down the rope onto the boat. One of the marines landed on the bow while the other landed on the stern, kneeling to break the momentum of their fall. Back on their feet, they discarded the rope and turned out their guns, holding the weapons at eye level, ready for any surprises. The howling wind and the noise from the choppers made the boat look more suspicious than it actually was.

The marine on the bow moved inward till he was under the thatch of hay, cutting out the uneasy sun. As he scanned the boat, he saw a body lying face down in the midst of the sunken deck. He signalled to his partner to move in together from both sides.

One marine adopted a defensive stance with his gun still trained on the body as he moved closer. Slowly he pushed the body with one hand and it rolled over. It was an aged Chinese male wearing a torn shirt and black trousers. The marine knew the drill and immediately went for the pulse under the unconscious man's chin. Nothing. He tried to press harder on the neck for any sign of life but the man had been dead for much longer than he expected. He signalled the result to his partner and slowly moved away to another part of the boat. They searched the entire boat for other clues. One marine stumbled upon the EPIRB—a small orange ball with a thin antenna rising a metre from the centre—neatly concealed under a wooden log. The marine turned off a small black switch at the base of the set, killing the transmission, and the small red light on top of the unit went out.

Meanwhile the other marine took out a small high-tech digital camera from his backpack, and pointing it at the dead man's face clicked a few photographs. He waited for a few seconds before pressing the 'Send' button on the back of the unit.

Both the marines went back to their landing position, holding the rope as one of the soldiers pressed the radio on his ear to update the pilot, 'We have a dead body here. Middle-aged Chinese male, probably been dead for more than 12 hours. No signs of any external wound. Rest of the boat is clean, no visible clues. I've sent you the photographs.' He spoke with a typical American accent.

'Yeah, I got the photographs alright. Not quite what we expected. Anyway, hang on men, I'm gonna make you fly.' The pilot replied as the marines were lifted off the boat onto the chopper.

~

Carlos sat intrigued by the chain of events, waiting for the Captain to come back online. Before long, a voice crackled, 'Inspector, we got ourselves a dead man. Anything you can tell me about this? I'm sending you pictures my men took. Take a look, maybe you can save me some time.'

Carlos rushed to the computer screen to see images of General Lee lying lifeless on the boat deck. Now there were more questions than he had expected and everyone turned to him for answers which he didn't have. All roads seem to lead to one man, Captain Murthy. Only he could provide the answers.

Carlos walked back to his office where Roberto and AJ were going through a bunch of files trying to figure out General Lee's role in the disappearance of the *Castle*. He looked at Roberto, 'Inform the UN Security Council immediately. Lee's death is a confirmation of AJ's news. If nuclear secrets are floating around, we have to act before they land in the wrong hands. Tell them to keep the coalition forces on standby. If we do find our rat, we won't have the time to wait for the pointless approvals from a hundred countries. We'll have to act before they expect it.'

Roberto left immediately to carry out the orders.

Turning to AJ, Carlos said sombrely, 'AJ, I want you to study every lead we have, every clue, even the smallest.'

'Alright, I'm on it,' AJ replied as he started to exit.

'We all meet here at midnight. No time to waste,' Carlos said.

AJ nodded, then left.

11

The Plot Thickens

It was 11:55 p.m. on the huge wall clock. The investigators had gathered in Carlos's office before time, with every bit of information they could lay their hands on. They looked like worn-out, yet excited, marathon runners on their last lap, except that they had many more laps to cross.

Carlos gathered a bunch of sheets scattered on his table. The investigators had a lot of clues but nothing substantial. Nothing on that desk lead them to what they were looking for. Who was selling that nuclear data, to whom, where and when? There were too many unanswered questions. Carlos had never come across a case of this scale. The involvement of so many nations and authorities had thrown in more knots than he could untie. His office was silent, disturbed only by the raindrops beating against the large window. Suddenly there was a knock on the door.

'Yes.' Carlos shouted without moving from his seat.

A middle-aged woman from the communication room stepped in. The tall and slim Latin American with dark skin and straight hair, elegantly dressed in semi-formals, held a sheet of paper. 'Inspector, we just received an email addressed to you. It came on the common server. I think you should take a look.'

'Who is it from?' Carlos asked.

'From Kin Lee. It came from a public café in Rizhao, China,' said the woman.

Roberto sprung up from his seat and snatched the paper from her. Everybody gathered around Carlos as he signalled her to leave. Roberto read the mail aloud:

Inspector Carlos,

If you are reading this message, then I'm long dead. Consider this a favour or the revenge of a murdered man, but whatever I tell you is important for you and me. About the Castle *hijacking, you are right about the Captain's involvement, but as you know, he could not have done it alone or without a purpose. Murthy was working for me. I could have made him a millionaire but looks like he wants more than he can digest. I believe he has sided with the Yakuza and was plotting to kill me. If they get their hands on the data, all hell will break loose. Stop them before it is too late. They are a dangerous lot. You will find the ship about 50 miles northeast of Puerto Rico at noon tomorrow along with all the proof you need.*

Regards
Kin Lee

As Roberto finished reading the email, words like 'Yakuza,' 'data,' 'too late,' 'dangerous lot,' raced through everyone's mind. General Lee had not mentioned anything about any nuclear data but he referred to information which was potentially dangerous.

'There is certainly something other than the ship that the man sold,' Roberto spoke, breaking the silence.

'Yes, it's like a confirmation of what my sources said. Nuclear technology, that's what he's selling!' AJ's eyes gleamed with excitement.

'You're right, it does strengthen that premise but there is no clear reference in General Lee's email,' Carlos said pensively.

'True, but we don't have an option. Whatever this data is, it is important enough for someone to have him killed. If that is true, then we have to act now,' Carlos seemed to convince himself more than the others in the room.

'There's no time for procedures. I mean we have to involve everybody—Brazil, Panama, India, Puerto

Rico, China, the US and God knows who else!' Roberto sounded impatient.

Carlos ran the whole story in his head. Then he look at Roberto and said, 'Inform everybody involved. Tell them it's Code Red. We'll do a briefing in the conference hall in an hour. Looks like a dead man is solving our case.'

Roberto and AJ left the room to prepare for the high-profile meeting.

~

Carlos had escaped death twice. He thought of those times as he waited in his office for Roberto.

Fifteen years ago, a charming young officer stepped out of his patrol car and bravely walked up to the entrance of a small suburban house. The mesh door was locked from inside. Carlos was there to question a suspect in a murder case. He knocked on the door loudly a couple of times and waited to be let in. Suddenly a bullet tore through the mesh, grazing his ear. It took Carlos some time to realise he was still alive, and to take the culprit to task.

A decade back, Carlos had locked horns with Brazil's most notorious criminal whom he had given heroic chase till he found himself alone in the wilderness without a third person in sight, with a fully loaded classic revolver pointed at his head. The finger at the trigger was that of a criminal who was in a mood for some Russian roulette. As Tro slowly pulled the trigger, Carlos realised that being in heaven took more than a split second, he was still alive.

Now he snapped back to reality once again. Roberto walked in and said, 'Everybody's here, they are going to the conference hall now. Are you ready?'

'I'm always ready!' Carlos smiled as he got up from the seat, put on his coat and patted his messed up hair back in place.

As both of them walked briskly towards the hall, Carlos enquired, 'Who all do we have here?'

'Well, we have summoned all the parties whose approvals are required to act on this. Other than our people, we have the Defence Attachés of China, Panama, India, the US, Curaçao, Japan and Puerto Rico,' he replied, counting on his fingers. 'And yes, people from the UNSC. They have to get the paperwork done at supersonic speed.'

Deep down, Carlos knew this would be tougher than he was expecting. He pushed open the door and walked into a moderate-sized conference hall, with Roberto feeding him every last bit of information he would need for the high-profile briefing. The oval-shaped hall was well lit. One of the assistants placing mineral water bottles on the round table stood at attention as he saw the chief walk in. Carlos gave him a quick smile without saying anything and the assistant went back to his job.

AJ was followed by the entire group of representatives Roberto had mentioned earlier. The group looked larger than Carlos had expected, and had more men than women. AJ was accompanied by the commissioner of police and a few more high-profile officials from Rio. Assistants ushered them to their seats.

The commissioner of police took his seat next to Carlos who was still standing, waiting for his guests to settle down.

'Alright Carlos, this better be good,' said the commissioner of police.

'Good morning, ladies and gentlemen. I am sorry to have disturbed you at this hour but the situation called for urgent action requiring approvals and clearances from countries represented by all those present here,' said Carlos. 'Without wasting any more time, I'll get to the point. Six days ago, MV *Castle* went missing off Curaçao along with the Master. The crew, however, was signed off safely by people they thought were the agents for the vessel. What we initially believed to be a hijacking turned out to be a well-executed theft.

'Our investigations have indicated the involvement of the Master on the ship at that time, Captain Murthy, in this scam, but there are larger players as well.' Carlos paused, before continuing. 'In another development, our intelligence has information that sensitive nuclear data could illegally exchange hands in the next few days.'

His last words woke up everyone in the hall. A representative looked deeply disturbed, 'Inspector, how are these two related?'

'Well, they are,' Carlos replied calmly. 'We have not been able to identify the source and nature of this nuclear data as yet, but there are many indications of movement of large sums of money in the past few days. Mostly from China and Japan.' He said this without looking at the respective representatives.

'General Kin Lee, from China, was possibly involved in the sale of the data. The point of concern is that all leads in the *Castle* case point to the same person. We believe that someone was probably selling this information to the Japanese mafia in the guise of a ship but again we have no concrete evidence.

'General Lee was found murdered on a boat off Panama. The rescue operation was conducted by the American coastguard. And a few hours back, we received an email from this dead man, in which he has owned up to being for a kingpin in this scam and has claimed that Captain Murthy along with the Japanese mafia were planning to assassinate him.'

He clicked a button on the remote in his hand and the email he had received was projected on the wall behind him. All eyes were fixed on it. Everyone looked stunned. Some reached for their cell phones to inform the concerned ministries in their respective countries about the gravity of the situation.

'Maybe they can give us some insight?' Carlos said, pointing at the Chinese representative.

The man was taken by surprise and looked slightly embarrassed. Then he cleared his throat and said, 'We did find some movement of funds in General Lee's account in the past few days but it's not easy to track the accounts of such people. Gathering enough information to be able to question them requires time and effort.'

Carlos intervened. There was a sense of urgency in his voice, 'The only thing that we are short of is time. As of now, we cannot say that the information in this letter is 100 per cent accurate, but I don't think we have any other option. If the ship is actually going to be off Puerto Rico with all that data this morning, then we have to act fast to secure it either through persuasion or by force. To do that, I need a go-ahead from all of you. And since we don't have the time to make adequate preparations from here, we would need the assistance of the UN security forces.' Carlos placed the remote back on the table.

The answer was clear in everyone's head, but the legalities were enormous and nobody was willing to take the lead.

'If this deal does go through, as planned and leads to a catastrophe in some part of the world, you don't want to be thinking for the rest of your life that you could have saved thousands of lives, but didn't,' Carlos ended his brief.

Some representatives talked among themselves for a few seconds and then said, 'We need some time to give the go-ahead.'

'Thank you very much,' replied Carlos. The situation had put everyone in a difficult spot.

Nearly everyone left the hall and was busy making calls. After a string of calls and intense discussions that seemed to last hours, it was decided unanimously that Code Red was ready to be executed.

'Alright gentlemen, it's official. The operation will be conducted by the UN security forces under your guidance. Act carefully and responsibly and remember, the whole world will be watching,' the commissioner of police was preparing his men mentally and emotionally for yet another difficult task.

~

A few miles from the headquarters, Ricardo sat in a small and moderately furnished room, holding his face in his hands. The walls were grimy and the furniture seemed good enough to discard. A table lamp gave off a dim haunting glow.

Ricardo sat staring at the clock as one hand moved sluggishly to the next minute. Things had not turned out as he had planned. The image of Carlos sitting in front of him in the small interrogation room kept flashing through his head.

'Once the ball starts rolling, there won't be any turning back,' Carlos had said.

'Look around you, Carlos. The ball is already rolling,' Ricardo had retorted.

The pounding on the door reeled Ricardo back to reality. He looked at the clock. It was half past three. He got up slowly and moved towards the door, telling himself as he opened it, 'No more turning back now.'

12

USD 2 Billion

As Carlos sat surrounded by military experts and strategists, in another part of the world the sun was rising above the horizon. But something in the air that day forebode gloom. The sky was bereft of the usual splash of colours, and the air was still. An overwhelming sense of defeat loomed large as the hours ticked by. Tro stepped out of his black Audi at the wharf as the *Trader* stood tame behind him, and the sun shone on the massive ship, casting a deep shadow on the foreground. Today was the big day, the day he had looked forward to for a long time. He was joined by his bodyguards and Caster and they walked steadily towards a group of four Japanese men standing where the gangway of the *Trader* met the wharf.

'Good morning gentlemen, welcome to Montserrat,' Tro said as he shook hands with an elderly man in the group. Kamai Yokogawa was one of the lead operatives of the Yakuza.

'Good morning to you too, it's a pleasure to finally meet you Mr. Tro,' Yokogawa replied in English with a pronounced Japanese accent.

'The pleasure's all mine,' Tro replied with a warm smile as he signalled one of his bodyguards who stepped forward with a green briefcase. Tro stood still and waited. The bodyguard now held the briefcase up for him to open. Tro punched in a digital code.

The Japanese looked intrigued and leaned forward to see what was in the briefcase. Tro turned back to the curious group, smiling as he removed his shaded glares and placed them in the breast pocket.

After a long beep, followed by a clicking sound, the briefcase sprung open. Inside a small black hard drive was fixed in the centre with clips. Tro gave the curious visitors only a glimpse of the intriguing drive and pressed the case shut as he turned to Yokogawa and said sternly, 'This is my part of the bargain. Your bit now.'

Yokogawa signalled the man standing behind him. Immediately the man pulled out his phone and dialled a number.

'Transfer the amount.' Then turning to Tro, he said, 'Your money is on its way Mr. Tro.'

Caster was by Tro's side in a jiffy, and punched a few keys on a small laptop. He had logged into their newly created account in the National Bank of Switzerland to check the balance. After an agonisingly long minute, a message appeared, 'New transfer received. USD 2,000,000,000.00

Suddenly Tro looked relaxed. Caster verified the final credit one last time before transferring the money to another account. Within seconds, the sum had travelled half the globe. Caster gave Tro a nod when all was done and shut the laptop.

'Alright gentlemen, it's been a pleasant transaction,' Tro announced as he handed over the briefcase to the Japanese. 'A map with the route out of here has been placed on the bridge. The safest way out is to go north till you pass Anegada and then proceed west to about 50 miles north of St. Juan. What you do after that is totally your business.'

'Thank you for everything. It has been a pleasure doing business with you. I hope we don't have to meet in this regard again,' Yokogawa replied bluntly.

'I'm sure we'll never meet again,' Tro replied.

Minutes later, his men were pulling the ropes off the bollards, casting off the *Trader.* The rechristened vessel shattered the peace of the surroundings with a long deafening sound of its air horn as it turned away from the jetty to commence her next passage.

Tro put on his glares once again to cut out the bright sun and the departing vessel. As he stepped into his car, a group of young flight engineers at the UN air base in Puerto Rico opened the life-size gate of the central hangar, revealing three fully-loaded stealth operation choppers.

13

The Countdown Begins

Carlos was surrounded by a group of men dressed in military uniforms as he tried to fight off his fears. The huge room, closed on all sides, with just a steel door which could only be opened by a retina scan, was filled with computers and projectors. The wall in front of him was lined with giant screens from ceiling to floor. A row of computers faced the screens, each unit manned by an operator from the forces. Papers and files were piled up on the tables. There was a touch screen control in the centre of the room. This was the command centre of the special operations cell and the officer with them was Sergeant Savio Fernandez.

Everyone pored over the plans spread out on the table. Suddenly someone stepped in. Major Ming Leong Ki, a South Korean, represented the UN security force. Everybody was taken aback by the quiet entry, but then quickly went back to the task at hand. Intelligence agencies across the globe had spent the night preparing a strategy for the day to come. Ki had great experience in disaster management and was considered one of the best strategists by many of these agencies.

'It looks ok, I guess. The secret for a fool proof plan is to be prepared for the worst. We have no idea how heavy the resistance will be, but we are going in prepared for the worst.' Ki sounded like a philosopher.

'What about the exact coordinates of the encounter?' Fernandez asked. 'We will use four choppers to carry out a parallel search in the MPA till the target is acquired. Once we have them in sight, the choppers will regroup 20 miles ahead and prepare for the showdown.' Ki replied confidently.

'When do we start the search?' Carlos asked.

'They fly at nine.' He replied, almost as a mystic.

~

The *Trader* was making its way through the calm seas, unaware of the dangers that stalked her passage. The decks were empty as members of the Yakuza rested in their cabins. They were heavily armed with automatic weapons, although they believed they had already won. Yokogawa stood on the bridge in front of a small laptop as one of his technical experts took out the hard drive, and placed it on a small mat on the table next to the computer. Linking the drive to the USB connection, he waited for the screen to appear. After a few seconds, a disclaimer popped up stating all the legal implications of viewing the data contained on the drive. The operator gave Yokogawa a smile as he pressed the 'Accept' button on the screen. Immediately another screen sprung up.

'Extracting data. Estimated time remaining: 170 minutes.'

Both bystanders moved a few inches closer to the screen for a look at the information that had just appeared.

'Looks like it will take some time,' the operator spoke.

Yokogawa frowned as he walked away. Impatience gnawed at his entrails, more so when a deal came with the price tag of USD 2 billion.

'Keep me informed.'

~

Ki and his team watched excitedly as the large screens in front of them came alive with maps, schedules, and photographs of the Puerto Rican military base and the adjoining waters, with the most probable areas of the air search marked in different colours and patterns.

A video popped up in one corner as a well-built, young man in a jumpsuit appeared on the screen. The video now displayed a fully loaded chopper and some flight technicians running around for the final preparations.

'Good morning Captain,' Ki greeted the man in the video.

'Good morning, sir.'

'Gentlemen, this is Squadron Leader Mark Ranger. He will be heading the choppers to the mission,' Ki added.

Turning back to the screen, he continued, 'You already have the plan, no changes. The target is expected to be at the LZ around noon but we will carry out an MPA search as planned. We expect them to be armed and dangerous, which is why the whole squad has been summoned. Captain, we have to secure the data.'

He pressed a button on the pad and Yokogawa's photograph appeared on the screen.

'This is Kamai Yokogawa. According to our intelligence sources, currently the ship is under his command and must I remind you that these people are armed and dangerous. You should expect heavy resistance.'

Ranger nodded.

'Captain, are your men ready?' Ki asked.

'Sir! They are all loaded and ready to roll. Give us the signal and we'll go kick some Japanese ass,' Ranger replied with a smile.

'Alright then, your choppers leave base with full arsenal at 0900 local time. Best of luck, Captain. I hope to see you in one piece after this,' Ki spoke with a mix of concern and confidence as he gave the final orders.

'Sir, what about the crew?' Ranger asked casually before leaving.

'Expendable.' He replied harshly as the screen went blank.

Ten minutes later, four choppers loaded with marines lined with full arsenal took off from the Puerto Rican air base, and tore their way across the clear sky towards the LZ as Carlos and Roberto stood with their fingers crossed at the command centre.

As the *Trader* came closer to the point of 'abandon ship,' the pop-up screen showed 50 minutes to go.

~

Yokogawa stood on the edge of the bridge wing as the breeze swept through his hair. The operator bowed as a mark of respect.

'It should be done any time now,' he tried to sound reassuring.

Soon the timer would be down from 50 minutes to zero. The Yakuza rode the seas preparing to rule the world but oblivious to the skies. On the bridge wing of the *Trader,* Yokogawa's impatience got the better of him, and he decided to call Tro on his cell phone to banter with him, rather against the convention of such deals. The operator replied that the number was out of coverage area. Yokogawa chucked the phone on a deck chair. Before he could think of what to do next, two of his men armed with automatic weapons sprinted to the wing.

'Yoko San, military choppers coming in.' They pointed at four small stealth birds in the distance.

Yokogawa's face turned pale. He ordered his men to take position and ran inside closing the door behind him.

A few miles ahead, the choppers hovered close to the waters, waiting for the *Trader* to steam in but something seemed wrong. Ranger saw the ship slowing down and turning into the wind on his radar. Immediately, he contacted the command centre where Ki stood standby for any abnormality. 'Base, this is Eagle one, the ship seems to be stopping two miles short of the LZ, over.'

Ki, composed till now, was taken by surprise.

'Shit, Eagle one, I think you have been spotted. Captain, move in and secure the data, I repeat secure the data, over,' he shouted.

'Roger on that, we are proceeding to secure the data, Eagle one over and out,' Ranger replied, as he hung up and under his command all the choppers started to gain altitude as they proceeded towards the *Trader* lying dead in the sea a few miles away.

Within minutes the choppers hovered around the *Trader* and took position for the attack, the noise of their huge engines paralysing Yogokawa's senses. While two choppers steadied in front of the bridge on each side, the other two swung back covering each quarter.

A bunch of the Yakuza came to the bridge wings, armed with automatic weapons and took positions behind the bulwark, aiming their weapons at the enemy. The choppers now flew at eye level, only metres away from the wings, as the marines took positions. Each chopper had a mounted machine gun on one side and marines with sniper rifles on the other. They were ready to take down any offensive.

Ranger had to follow international laws before engaging in combat, so he switched on the speaker. 'This is the UN security force. Lay down your weapons and surrender.'

The gunmen on the bridge did not move. One of them pressed the trigger, firing a shot at one of the Eagles.

All Ranger needed was a mistake from the opponents. Without wasting a single second, he pressed his radio and ordered his unit. 'Weapons free.'

Two fishermen on a small boat, drifting a few miles away, watched as the choppers opened fire from all sides, tearing apart every bit of what was left of the *Trader*, once the majestic MV *Castle*.

The noise of the gunfire had everybody on their toes at the command centre. Carlos stood staring at the big screen showing feeds of dying men from cameras mounted on the choppers as a few fell on the decks while the rest jumped overboard in the last bid to save their lives. Ki was running in every direction, clutching a radio and instructing the assailants on their next move as Fernandez followed him.

As two teams of fully-loaded marines landed on either side of the bridge, a bullet tore through the side glass and met Yokogawa in his chest taking him to the ground. With no hope of escape, Yokogawa closed his eyes to his dream of bringing the world down on its knees.

14

Yet Another Killing

As the bloodshed continued on the *Trader*'s deck, Tro walked into a private terminal in Montserrat. Caster came running towards him to take his briefcase. They waited in front of the glass door. A security guard in a Black Cat Commando get-up hurried to the digital lock on the other side and punched in a code. The door slid open. Tro didn't wait for any conversation and walked through. Caster followed him silently. The guard gave them a half salute as they walked past. They had to get out of there as soon as possible.

As they reached the sun-swept runway, Tro looked at Caster.

'Have you cleaned up?'

'Every bit of it, there is no witness or evidence on this island,' Caster replied promptly.

'Where is he?'

Without saying anything, Caster pointed a finger at a mid-sized private plane standing a few yards away. Near the boarding ladder, Murthy stood nattily dressed in a black suit against the silver of the aircraft. Tro raised his hand in greeting and Murthy responded warmly.

'Congratulations Captain, time to celebrate,' Tro said as they boarded the flight. Caster followed them in. It was time to propose a toast—to the success of their operations.

Murthy was touched by Tro's hospitality. Till a few days ago, he was leading a rudderless existence, and now he was in a multi-million dollar aircraft with more in his pockets than he could have ever dreamt of.

Minutes later, the plane took off from Montserrat.

~

The shattered remains of the *Trader* clung to the anchor as she rode the swell in vain. The dying sun bled shades of red and orange in the skies. A few military boats floated around the *Trader*, with photographers and detectives taking every bit of evidence that was left. The whole area had been cordoned off to avoid undue media hype. On the deck of the *Trader* stood Ranger with a satellite phone pressed to his ear as he briefed Ki at the other end.

'That is correct. We have found the drive. The data would have been a boon for rogue nations and terrorists across the world.'

'Alright, gather all evidence that you can find. Leave nothing behind,' Ki ordered.

Carlos stood still. He was busy contemplating all possibilities.

'What about Murthy?' Carlos asked suddenly.

'What?' Ranger questioned, seemingly lost in the call.

'What about Murthy, the Captain?' Carlos repeated his question.

'Any sign of the Master?' Ki asked Ranger.

'Nothing here, we searched the entire area. Nor has he drowned. He's not here.'

Ki turned to Carlos who stood lost in thought. 'So much for now, Inspector. I'll send you the files tomorrow,' Ki consoled Carlos.

'Tomorrow will be too late,' Carlos replied as he rushed out of the room to meet Roberto and AJ who were waiting for him outside. Carlos walked up to them and the three went into a huddle. While AJ looked deeply disturbed, Roberto seemed more composed and focused.

'Now what?' Roberto enquired in a hushed tone.

'What? You saw that drive they recovered. The Japanese were all over that little box. It's not the ship they bought. It was that drive which contained nuclear data. And our main man is still missing, they couldn't find him there,' Carlos replied, sounding tired.

'Either this man is too smart or too bloody dumb. I'm not even sure if he's alive or buried in some unknown graveyard,' said AJ.

'Oh, he isn't dead. In a single day, the most wanted Chinese and Japanese cartels are dead because of one man. He is smarter than we had expected,' Carlos replied.

'At least we found the ship. That was our case after all,' Roberto tried to see the brighter side of life.

'That's right, but the case is not closed. We need Murthy, dead or alive, to pack this one.' Carlos walked towards the exit. 'Let's get out of here.'

His two mates followed, trying to keep pace with him.

A moonless night descended on Rio. The air was still and the temperature had dropped to a comfortable low. They walked up to Carlos's car, a shining black Porsche SUV with a red siren on the roof, parked a few metres from the entrance. Carlos rested his weight against the dark rider.

'With the ship in our hands, we can easily silence the media. They'll forget about Murthy in no time,' Roberto suggested.

'Yes, but sooner or later, the missing man will be back in focus. We need to find him before anybody else does, and right now there is only one man who can tell us where Murthy could be,' Carlos replied.

'Ricardo?' AJ wondered.

'Ricardo. Maybe he was right. Murthy might want him dead,' Carlos confirmed. He immediately pulled out his cell phone and dialled a number. Then he heard the ring at the other end.

A few kilometres away stood the police safe house with all lights turned off and just one lamp burning futilely inside the small check post outside. The phone in the small cabin kept ringing. No one answered it.

Carlos waited for sometime till he realised something was amiss. Without wasting a second, he jumped into the car and hit the ignition. Roberto and AJ followed him. Carlos stepped on the gas as hard as he could and turned on the siren. They hit the main road, negotiating a sharp turn at high speed. The whole car tilted to one side as Roberto held on to the dashboard to hold his balance. The car sped past a red light barely missing a small sedan. Carlos threw the phone at Roberto, keeping his eyes on the road as he took another sharp turn.

'Keep trying,' he shouted.

Roberto obeyed and kept calling the number again and again with no response. AJ who was crouched in the backseat wondered what was going on. They took another sharp turn off the highway and came onto a half-laid rubble road. Carlos kept the accelerator pressed as they tore through the wilderness, leaving behind a cloud of dust. They could see the safe house ahead of them with all the lights turned off.

Carlos pulled up in front of the main entrance, turning off the siren and the engine at the same time. Everybody jumped out, their service weapons in hand.

Carlos motioned AJ to go to the check post while he proceeded towards the entrance accompanied by Roberto, with their guns close to their chest.

AJ opened the cabin door slowly to find the guard lying unconscious in his chair. A strange smell in the cabin indicated foul play. AJ knew the guard wasn't sleeping, he had fallen unconscious. He checked the guard's pulse and to his relief, all seemed well. Quietly, he stepped back and moved out towards the rear of the safe house.

Roberto slowly turned the knob of the main door, clicking it open noiselessly. He walked into the house stealthily with Carlos just behind him. They entered a small room with a folding bed in the centre and old furniture in the corners. Carlos tried to switch on the light, but the power lines had been disconnected. Slowly they fanned out to the other rooms, anticipating an encounter.

There was no sign of life. Meanwhile, AJ managed to locate the main switchboard in the backyard and fixed the fuse. Inside Carlos and Roberto jumped to their feet as the lights came on. Without exchanging a word they searched all the rooms, upturning old furniture for hidden clues. Suddenly Carlos spotted a blood-stained jacket in a corner. He had seen Ricardo wearing it often. The carpet looked as though a body had been dragged across it before the blood stains mysteriously disappeared at the door. As Roberto joined him, they stood motionless staring at what looked like the remains of a murder site.

AJ entered from the back door holding his gun, and relaxed when he saw his companions in a corner. He walked across to them only to be shocked himself.

'Shit!' He exclaimed.

Carlos put his gun back into the holster and declared, 'Ricardo may already be dead. And Murthy may have already escaped our clutches.'

15

The Grenadines

Off the coast of the Grenadines—a small atoll among the Windward Islands in the Caribbean Sea—a luxury yacht drifted lazily, lost somewhere between Grenada and Saint Vincent Islands. Spotless white from keel to mast, its black window shades added to its allure.

As the sun rose, the chirping of birds throttled the silence of the skies. The bay was lined with sail boats and expensive cruisers parked neck to neck for the rich and powerful from around the world. Ricardo stepped into the luxury yacht at the marina. The yacht was a pricstly white with black glass windows. A spotless steel railing lined the open deck. Ricardo wore a white casual shirt with floral prints across one shoulder and a pair of blue trousers. His aviators covered most of his face, blocking off unwelcome light. As he closed the door to his cabin, he was taken aback by a sudden intrusion. He jumped back pulling out a small gun that he had slipped into his shirt, holding it at eye level. To his relief, it was Tro dressed in off-white from head to toe. Immediately Ricardo's frown transformed into a hesitant smile as he placed the gun on a side table and walked up to Tro.

'Marco,' Ricardo whispered repeatedly like a medium in a trance. Ricardo had dreamt of this day since his childhood. Every night in the orphanage, he would go to bed, hoping Marco would come the next day to take him home and envelope him in the warmth of his protective hug.

Marco, the man wanted by every intelligence agency in the world, the master of deceit, held Ricardo, his cousin, tightly as tears welled up in his eyes. The only family each had was the other.

Ricardo slowly let himself go. He shut his eyes, reminiscing his days as a little boy in the small house in Recife, sitting on the shelf of the open kitchen with young Marco cooking for both of them.

Once Marco had forgotten how hot the stove was and had burnt his hand.

'Does it hurt?' Ricardo had asked innocently, trying to feel Marco's pain.

Marco had smiled at the little boy. 'There are things you need to forget in life. Pain is one of them.'

'And the other things?'

Suddenly Ricardo snapped out of his lost childhood and returned to the day he had woken up to the strange call on a Sunday morning.

'Hello…' he had said lazily.

'Ricardo, is that you?' It was Marco speaking softly.

'Yes, who is this?'

'It's Marco.'

Ricardo hadn't known what to say or how to react. Just ten minutes of conversation between the two cousins could not have erased years of loneliness and destitution within the confines of the orphanage at Recife. Forgiveness and healing was a long way off.

Marco had then told him about his plans for the *Castle*. At first Ricardo had been reluctant to pawn his soul to his brother, but as he mulled over the proposition, he realised for years he had been looking to escape from a thankless life, and perhaps, this was the only way out, as terrible as it seemed. Twenty-four hours later Ricardo was ready to walk the road to perdition that Marco had led him on.

Today, Ricardo took rapid stock of his life. 'These last few days I've been sent to jail, almost got caught, almost got killed and now the world thinks I'm dead.'

Marco put his arm around Ricardo's shoulders.

'Things don't always pan out according to formula. On the brighter side, you're the only family I have. And the important thing is that you are safe and free.'

He winked at Ricardo. Then Marco picked up the gun lying on the side table and placed it firmly in Ricardo's hand. 'Murthy is on his way, you know what to do.'

Ricardo nodded. This was something he didn't have to do, but this was something that he was going to do. It was the last step that would take him beyond heaven and hell.

~

Eyes shut, Murthy lay indolently on a sunbathing chair on the front deck of the luxury yacht. 'I deserve it,' he smiled smugly as he indulged in an internal monologue.

He had done it. An impossible idea till a month ago, he had accomplished it now. Suddenly a familiar voice disrupted the calm.

'Sleeping, Captain?'

Ricardo stood tall, his body pushed against the bulkhead outside the cabins. A faint smile played on his lips as he introduced the distraction.

'You!' Murthy exclaimed in disbelief as he scrambled to get up. 'How...?' All of a sudden his moment of victory seeped out of him. Confused words tumbled out of his lips. 'You? Here? But how?'

Ricardo let out a laugh. The creases on Murthy's forehead deepened.

'It's a small world, Captain,' Ricardo said grimly, as he pulled out a mini Biretta skillfully concealed in his shirt. Slowly he took aim at the enemy's heart. It was time to act, time to emerge from his cocoon. Without giving Murthy time to react, Ricardo pulled the trigger. He felt a crushing jolt at his shoulder as the bullet emerged from the barrel and flew swiftly towards Murthy, meeting his torso just above his heart, setting free the dark blood inside into an even darker world outside.

Murthy's eyes remained fixed on Ricardo, searching for an answer. Something told him this was the end. 'Why me? Why this fate?' As life ebbed out of him through the bloody window of injured flesh, the dying man desperately sought answers. Seconds later, a gasping Murthy fell on the white deck blighting it with a red pool.

A man appeared behind Ricardo, his face visible to the near-corpse. Murthy took his eyes off his killer and turned his gaze upon the newcomer. How remarkably similar the two faces in front of him were. An anguished laugh escaped his dry lips as a final convulsion wrenched the last dregs of life out of him.

Ricardo stared at the lifeless body. Sorrow and pain set in. Along with Murthy he had killed another soul—the Ricardo he had known all his life, the Ricardo who hated life at the orphanage, but loved the footfall fields and beaches of Recife. Still unsure of how to react to his own actions, a million unanswered questions cruised through his head. Suddenly everything around him seemed very bright making it difficult for him to keep his eyes open. Then his gaze fell on the murderous weapon still in his hand. He felt his head spinning as he dropped the gun on the deck. He grabbed the rail with one hand to regain his senses. Before he could fully recover, an ear-shattering splash at the other end distracted him. Was he hallucinating?

On the edge of the rail, Marco stood indolently with his weight against the bulwark. He had just dumped Captain Murthy's corpse into the sea, wiping out with that, the last traces of an honest man easily corrupted.

Ricardo stared at the man standing on the edge so calmly. There was no guilt or remorse on Marco's face. If at all, he looked triumphant. Ricardo realised that he had played on the wrong side.

Standing at the edge of the forecastle, Ricardo stared at the waves breaking on the hull. He knew that someday, he would have to pay for his sins.

Marco walked up to Ricardo and put an arm around him. 'Life carries on Ricardo, despite everything.'

'This is not how it was supposed to be,' Ricardo replied, almost talking to himself.

'We did what was required. The bottom line is that you are here, safe.'

'You promised there would be no bloodshed,' Ricardo sounded remorseful.

'We did what was required. Is that too hard to understand? How much time and money I spent to make sure that we did not leave behind a trail. And if that required a few sacrifices along the way, I don't care and neither should you.'

For Ricardo, this explanation seemed inadequate.

Marco continued, 'A few days after your ship sailed from Brazil, Murthy got scared. Half way through the plan he wanted to quit. I called Daze and asked her to move ahead with the next plan. The second man with her, the Latino, was useless, a scum bag off the streets. We took him because he was expendable. I laid the bait for Murthy and he bit it. He had been hard to persuade when I had called him the first time.'

Jason had picked up the phone. 'Captain, there's a call for you.'

Murthy had come on the line and moved to one side to block out Jason.

'MV *Castle*, Captain speaking.'

'Good morning Captain. My name is Tro, consider me your friend.'

Murthy had listened attentively for almost 35 long minutes and finally hung up, confused about his principles.

'I'll call you tomorrow for your final word, Captain. Remember, if you don't do it, somebody else will. But I hope it's your account number I'll punch in at the end of it all,' Tro had said before hanging up.

After a sleepless night, Murthy had become a part of Tro's well-thought-out plan to sell the ship and along with that, the data that he had sourced from a top-notch scientist in the government's payroll. Murthy had helped the two stowaways board the *Castle* in Brazil when he deliberately kept the gangway unmanned by dispatching the watch to the engine room. Daze and her accomplice had boarded the vessel unnoticed before she sailed.

Murthy had been playing his role all along to keep the stowaways hidden even when Jason had almost spotted Daze in the provision store. The officers had carried out a search but Murthy had ensured they remained undetected.

'Who is it?' Ricardo had shouted on reaching the highest level in the cold Provision store.

Murthy had replied from the other corner, 'Nobody, it's just me. It's clear.'

Immediately Korpovich had spoken from the other end, 'Same here, not even a rat!'

Ricardo had looked into the two dark corners and shouted, 'Well then what are we waiting for, let's get out of here.'

Just as everybody had proceeded to the exit, Murthy had told the hidden stowaways,'Stay here for five minutes and then vanish,' before leaving to meet the rest of the group outside the store.

A few days later Murthy had called Tro.

'I can't do this. What if I get caught?' He had spoken like a man held back by his conscience.

'Relax, Captain. It's my job to make sure that nothing happens to you. Trust me. I'm watching every move carefully,' Tro had consoled him.

Murthy had hung up that day seemingly pacified but fear still lurked in his mind. Little did he know that Ricardo, Tro's man, had been watching every move he made, correcting any mistake that could jeopardise the master plan.

But that perhaps was not enough, and Tro was not going to take a chance. He had called Daze soon after his chat with Murthy. 'Hello darling. There's been a slight change of plans here. The caretaker seems to be in two minds. He's going to need some motivation from your end.' After an update from her on her part of the deal, Tro had said, 'Yes, let's go ahead with plan B, and keep me informed.'

Murthy blindly walked into the trap, killed the Latino and kept it a secret. Murthy had to become the culprit. The world was looking for the man who had the answers. But now he was dead and gone, taking with him all the names and secrets.

Ricardo stood staring at the deep sea as the soft breeze billowed out his shirt.

'You know if you stay out at sea for too long, these waters start to mess with your head. All you sailors have the same problem, whether you recognise it or not. These oceans make you evaluate everything in terms of good and bad, right and wrong. Well, the world doesn't function that way. You have to bend the rules and make compromises, stifle your conscience to get ahead in life. The sooner you realise that, the better for you. I mean isn't it evident? Look around you. Theft, piracy, terrorism. You guys are taking a beating everywhere. It's time to wake up, Ricardo, see the truth. The world is not how you want it to be.' Marco pummelled the railing as he vented his frustration.

Ricardo shut his eyes and took a deep breath. He would try forgetting all that had happened. When he set out from Recife, he didn't realise just how far he would have to travel out.

16

Reclamation

Ricardo slowly slid down the polished deck, resting his weight against the steel railings. He shut his eyes to cut off the bright sun. Memories of the Latino, Lee, Murthy began to haunt him. He could no longer figure out what was worse—the days gone by or the ones yet to come.

Marco's master plan had worked out just as he had wanted it to. The world was his chessboard and he played to win. Now with Yokogawa dead as well, all traces that could lead the cops to his door had been wiped clean. In fact, the investigators had themselves wiped out all witnesses who could have solved their case.

Suddenly Marco looked at Ricardo. 'You're alright?'

With a forced smile, Ricardo nodded. Both stood shoulder to shoulder looking at the beautiful waters beneath.

'Look around you Ricardo, we own the world,' Marco shouted at the top of his voice as Ricardo stood staring at his brother.

With time, news about the theft of the *Castle* faded as fresh scandals erupted in a confused world. All attention shifted to hotspots across the world where super powers, religious groups and terrorists indulged in a dogfight to prove a futile point. Marco took advantage of the situation to lay low for the storm to pass. Along with Ricardo, he hid in The Grenadines in a posh beach house surrounded with pure white sand. Coconut trees lining the beach swung gently in the breeze.

~

The sun had touched its low for the day as the skies lit up with stars. The off-white house, illuminated with little lamps, shone mystically by the moonlight. Ricardo and Marco sat at a teak dining table ringed with majestically carved chairs. The walls in the room were lined with paintings and contemporary pieces of art. The windows were dressed in heavy mauve curtains complementing the design on the ceiling.

Marco poured himself a glass of expensive Scotch. The alcohol started to raid his brain quietly. A life-size plasma screen mounted on the wall was turned on to a news channel. As they watched, a young female reporter rattled off: 'In a dramatic turn of events yesterday, UN security forces regained the control of the ship, MV *Castle* which had been hijacked almost a fortnight ago. There were no hostages and the only crew involved in the scam was the Indian Master onboard at the time of the incident, Captain Rajan Krishnamurthy. Acting on tip-offs from intelligence agencies, investigation units wasted no time in recapturing the ship. In what is being termed as a bloodbath by many, the Special Forces, in a joint operation, killed at least 20 members of the gang holding the vessel. The encounter took place off the island of Puerto Rico in the Caribbean Sea yesterday afternoon. The ship had been put in hiding in the Montserrat region and had sailed yesterday morning after being painted in a different colour. In a surprise and unexpected move, the forces apprehended the vessel in open water, killing all the culprits. The operation director has claimed that they were fired upon as they reached the vessel and their choppers returned fire in self-defence.

'The three member investigation team that has been probing the case is yet to make any statement and is awaiting final reports from the UNSC. The involvement of the Security Council is still unclear in this matter as officials prefer to remain silent on this issue. Though no official comment has been made, it is clear that the names behind the whole controversy have boiled down to the Chinese mafia and the Japanese Yakuza. As per initial reports, the international criminal court has placed Captain Rajan Krishnamurthy's name in the "most wanted" list. The only task the investigators have at hand now is to find the missing Captain.'

Before the reporter could get on with the next line, Marco turned off the television and laughed out loud. Running his hands through his hair, he turned to Ricardo.

'The world is too blinded by its own mess. Frankly, I would be surprised if they found out the truth. Like I said Ricardo, they see what they want to see. To rise in this world, all you have to do is see the obvious.' He seemed proud of his own deeds.

Ricardo sat unmoved by the speech his cousin had just made. As he stared at his cousin in the chair in front of him, he realised the depth of his deceit; beyond the shiny exterior, he saw darkness and dirt in his cousin's heart. It was too late for explanations. He sat quietly waiting for the right moment as Marco enjoyed his triumph.

'You seem quiet. What's wrong?' Marco said, intrigued by Ricardo's silence.

Ricardo was about to speak when the main door to the extreme end of the hall opened. Marco jumped to his feet. There were only two people in the house. No other company, not even security personnel. He had kept his location a secret, even from his own men.

Carlos walked in slowly shutting the door as he moved towards them. Dressed in a brown formal suit, he held a shiny Swiss revolver in one hand.

'Carlos!' Marco exclaimed 'How did you get here?'

While Marco stood in utter shock, Ricardo kept sitting calmly.

'Hello Ricardo!' Carlos said as he stopped a few steps short of the table.

'Good to see you, Carlos.'

'Ricardo, what is going on?' Marco shouted at the top of his voice.

'You were right, Marco. The sea does something to you. It makes you see the difference between right and wrong, good and evil. You abandoned me on the streets and left me to rot in that hell. And you thought I would go along with your plans?'

'I helped you get out of that miserable life of yours and this is how you repay me?' Marco was livid.

Ricardo said slowly, 'You needed me, that's why you called me and now that your work is done, sooner or later, you would have killed me too like you did the rest of them. I'm not like you, Marco. I killed Murthy to gain your trust so that I could reach here. I'm not like you.'

'I never thought of killing you, Ricardo. But now I know I made a mistake.' Marco replied. 'And this is your plan? Call Inspector Carlos to kill me. Do you think

I could have survived all these years without feeding the cops? Could I have gotten out of Brazil without Inspector Carlos's help?' Marco sneered at Ricardo.

Carlos, who was standing between the cousins, suddenly moved closer to Marco as his revolver shone mysteriously in Ricardo's eyes.

'I think there are some things you should know before you die. Carlos here has been a part of what you call my plans. I knew you couldn't be trusted. That's why I kept Carlos on your trail. How else do you think I managed to keep the cops off my doorstep?'

Ricardo looked unmoved by the revelation.

'Actually, I know.'

It was Marco's turn to be surprised. Ricardo went back to the day he was sitting in the small cell at the police headquarters in Rio.

Carlos looked at Ricardo for a minute. As he resolved his moral dilemma, he slowly shut the door and moved towards Ricardo. He walked up to the table and slowly positioned himself on the chair in front of Ricardo without taking his eyes off the target. He was trying to judge Ricardo's confidence while the man in front of him sat contemplatively.

'We're all part of the same game here, Carlos.' Ricardo spoke slowly. 'You thought you were clever, but even the smartest crooks make mistakes!' He added with a smile.

'What are you talking about?' Carlos was irritated.

'Come on, Carlos, admit it. You blew it. Calling Matt, Johan. You should be thankful Roberto didn't notice. But I did.'

After hearing Ricardo out, Carlos sat perplexed for a few minutes. Then his taut face broke into a shrewd smile.

'You're smart. So now what are you going to do? Tell the police, call Roberto?' he said mockingly.

'I know they won't listen, Carlos. I know that, but I want something only you can get for me.' Ricardo replied.

'What?'

Ricardo took a few seconds to think over what he was going to say. 'Marco.' He spoke in a whisper, hoping to somehow reclaim his damned soul.

Life was all about a change of heart—every second. At the extreme limit of greed lay the road back to life. Carlos was ready to walk back. He agreed to the plan.

'You just play along Carlos, leave the rest to me.' Ricardo spoke confidently.

'Once the ball starts rolling, there won't be any turning back.' Carlos said.

'Look around you,' said Ricardo. 'The ball is already rolling.'

Marco stood in shock as he looked at Ricardo.

'Carlos, you are my friend. After all these years of trust?' Marco hissed. 'How could you, you two-faced son of a...'

Carlos didn't give him time to complete his last words. Without warning he lifted the silver gun and with an unsteady aim, pressed the trigger. The bullet hit Marco in his chest.

Ricardo got up slowly from his chair, walked across to the lifeless corpse of his only family, before slumping to the floor.

'Let's get out of here, Ricardo.' Carlos helped him to his feet.

And as they left the room, Ricardo made a definitive break with his bloodline.

17

Tarragona and Sleep at Last

In the old town of Tarragona, night imposed darkness and silence on the streets. The city, dating back to before Christ, had witnessed great eras and the bloodiest extinctions. The narrow cobbled streets and the traditionally designed buildings stood unchallenged by time. The town held a typical European appeal, with the main street lined with pizzerias and cafés. At the end of the street stood a mammoth statue, like a sentinel, touching the sky above the open seas.

With stained glass windows and rock-cut walls, one of the cafés in Tarragona was full of period furniture and a bar at one end. On the small television, mounted on the wall, news was being spewed in Spanish, while English subtitles sprinted from one side of the screen to another. At one table, a solitary man casually sipped his coffee and listened to the updates from around the world.

'Another case, which had almost faded with time, is the controversial *Castle* robbery. Though the ship had been recovered a month ago, the police have still to trace the missing Captain Rajan Krishnamurthy. In an interesting letter submitted by the investigation team to the international court of justice, they have officially closed the case saying that their intelligence links reveal that Captain Rajan Krishnamurthy was killed a few days ago in Dubai. Though the body of the deceased has not been recovered, they have uncovered deposits worth USD 3 million in the name of the Captain. The money has been acquired during the illicit sale and the ship has been confiscated. The UN offshoot, IMO, has praised the three-member investigation team for their swift and timely resolution of this case.'

Ricardo was so engrossed in the news that he didn't notice that it was long past midnight. He got up quickly, leaving behind his last bills and coins for his meal on the table, and a generous tip for the waiter.

As he walked aimlessly on the deserted cobbled street, every noise around him became distinct. Lost in thought, he kept on walking. The incline increased further ahead, so he took a turn into a small street with the sign board saying 'Cathedral'. The lane was very narrow. The high walls on the sides were boundaries of old-style houses. The area was relatively dark with more shadows than light. Ricardo lost count of how long he had walked. He wanted to push his body and mind to the limits.

At the end of a long night, when he finally sank into his bed in a seedy motel, he drifted towards a dream he could never forget—on a foggy night, he was inches above the deep oceans, in the middle of his last fall, with his hands spread out, trying to catch the last spray of the breaking swell. And the ocean was parting to receive and cleanse him forever.